Paul Cox

THE ELEVENTH MAN

Llumina Press

ISBN: 978-1-62550-471-5

THE ELEVENTH MAN

CHAPTER ONE

THE ELEVENTH MAN

Squinting against the glare from under his tattered straw hat, a stoop shouldered man in faded overalls carefully studied the sheriff's office before stepping onto the Nevada interstate. Crossing over to the hardware store, he paused to spit a brown stream of tobacco onto the sidewalk, then pushed his way into the shaded entrance. "Anything happened, yet?" he asked.

A half-dozen older men stood leaning against a glass display cabinet; another, in an armless swivel chair, sat behind it at a cluttered desk. The man at the desk glanced up. "Don't think so, Digger," he answered, then went back to work cutting slices from a stick of salami with a pocketknife. Looking to the others, he said, "Not this fella."

"Oh, come on, Giz," protested a bystander. "He's not more than six feet and maybe one eighty-five."

"That's right, Giz, and Bob Muller's six-three and two-twenty, at least," chided another good-naturedly. "He weighed that much when he played for Nevada State, and being sheriff has kept him in good shape."

Giz Gibson shook his head and thumbed a piece of salami into his mouth. "Don't matter," he said, evenly.

The gray haired men on the other side of the counter chuckled.

"Did you hear, Digger?" grinned a hawk-nosed man with a missing front tooth. "Giz here is betting on the newcomer."

Digger Mosby thoughtfully scratched the tobacco stained whiskers beneath his lower lip. "You don't say. Why's that, Fred?"

"Giz was just about to tell us when you came in. Come on over here."

Digger eagerly took his place alongside the others, leaning his bony elbows on the thick glass. Catching the mood, he said wryly, "I can't wait to hear this!"

"Well, for one thing," drawled Gibson, as if half-interested, "I've sold him fifteen hundred creosoted posts in the last two months."

"What's that got to do with anything?" snapped Fred.

"I happen to know he's dug every one of them holes by hand and packed 'em with a six-foot steel rod," answered Gibson. "And he wasn't exactly frail when he first come in here, but he's already busting out of his shirts. That rod weighs a good forty pounds."

Digger nodded and pointed a greasy finger at Giz. "He's right about that. I been noticing the same thing at the station when he comes in to pump gas."

"That's not enough to take the sheriff," said Fred. "Remember what he done to that biker that come through here a couple of years ago? The one that took a swing at the sheriff? He beat that guy up with his bare fists so bad, he might have killed him if we hadn't of pulled him off."

"That's a fact," agreed Digger. "The good sheriff has a mean streak in him a mile wide, and he always has. Especially when it comes to outsiders. So, what else do you know about this new fella that makes you favor him in a fight?"

"First of all," muttered Giz, wiping his pocketknife on his pants, then snapping it shut. "That biker was big, but he was mostly fat. And second of all, I don't know much more about him than you all do. He don't talk much. Always pays up front, in cash, when he trades here, and I don't even know his last name—only Jason. Now, I may not know much from what he's told me, but I can see something about him…something I saw in the Viet Nam war."

Fred shook his head and smiled at those on either side of him. "Now, Giz, we was all in the war, too. What is it you see that we somehow can't?"

"I saw some like him in the infantry towards the end," answered Giz. "They were men that had been in the thick of it too long, and if you knew what was good for you, you stayed clear of them kind. If one of 'em ever let loose, it was like somebody opened up the gates of hell, and heaven help whoever got in their way."

Digger's eyes narrowed. "You saying he's crazy?"

"No!" scoffed Gibson, then took another bite of salami. After chewing it for several seconds, he continued. "I'm saying he's a man to stay clear of, that's all. You don't want to push him too far."

"Isn't that what you're all here for?" asked a scornful voice from the far end of the store, as a heavyset woman in her fifties worked her way forward, then back behind the counter. "I know why you're all loafing around town today and why you were doing the same thing last Saturday, too."

Fred smiled sheepishly at her, then replied politely, "Now, Matty, we just like to come visit you and Giz from time to time. And all of the sudden, you're getting suspicious of our good intentions."

Matty Gibson shook her head and shoved her hands down onto her hips. "Honestly!" she snapped. "That

Jason is a nice young man, and here you all are, hoping to see him and the sheriff get into a fight."

"We're not hoping," objected Giz. "We just figure it's gonna happen, and we don't want to miss it. That's all. And the way Bob's been on him, we figure today might be the day."

"Why doesn't the sheriff just leave him alone?" asked Matty. "That's all he wants. What did Jason ever do to Bob, anyway?"

Several of the men snickered, as one offered, "He bought Bob's ranch right out from under him, that's what."

"Bob doesn't have a ranch. Never has."

"That's right, Matty," explained Fred, delightfully. "Bob was saving up for the ranch next to the Whitney place, the Morgan ranch. I heard he almost had the down payment, when this new fella comes out of the blue and buys it up, and for cash money to boot."

Digger grinned knowingly, and elbowed Fred in the ribs. "And it's no secret how the sheriff feels about Kimberly Whitney, either. Word is he was hoping to impress Kimberly with his big deal and tell her when she got back. But now he can't do that, either, and he's fit to be tied."

Giz shrugged and looked up at his wife. "If Bob had offered a decent price for that property, instead of trying to get it for nothing, he wouldn't have a problem. He kept trying to outwait old Morgan, thinking nobody else would come along. Just outsmarted himself, Matty."

"The way I heard it," joined in Fred, "this Jason fella didn't dicker the price at all. He just asked how much and put down a cash deposit. Then two days later, he pays him the rest of it. He must be made out of money!"

"Who must be made out of money?" questioned a cheery voice from behind the cluster of men.

In unison, they turned to see a slender, sandy-haired young woman smiling at them, as she glanced up from a handful of mail. "What's this you've got here, a town meeting?"

With eyes darting from one to another, a round of mumbling and stammering broke out and continued, until Matty ended the chaos. "Welcome home, Kimberly. We didn't hear you come in. How was your trip?"

"Fine, thanks."

"And how is your Uncle John?"

"We had a good visit, but he's still trying to persuade me to move up to Colorado with him," answered the young woman, as she watched the elderly men disperse throughout the store. Turning to watch them meandering aimlessly among the shelves, she asked, "What was that all about?"

"Oh, it's a little involved," replied Matty disapprovingly, "but basically, they're just being men. They're hoping to see a fight or something. Heaven only knows."

"Things have livened up since I've been gone."

Matty lowered her head and squinted over a pair of half-rim glasses at the lightly freckled face and penetrating brown eyes across from her. "I think they'll liven up even more, now that you're back, Kimberly Whitney. It's your new neighbor that's causing all the excitement."

"You mean Morgan finally gave in and sold out?"

"Well—yes and no," answered Matty, obviously enjoying herself. "He didn't give in, but he did sell out."

"Are you saying Bob finally met his price?" asked Kimberly in surprise. "I didn't think he'd ever do that."

With a wrinkled brow, the older woman slid a pointed tongue past her upper lip. "It wasn't Bob who bought that property, Kimberly. It was a young man named Jason—a single, very polite, and very handsome young man."

Kimberly took a step back, then skeptically cocked her head to one side. "What?"

"That's right, Kimberly," agreed Giz, deciding it was safe to return to the counter. "And the sheriff's been on his back for one thing or another ever since."

For a moment, Kimberly was silent, then, after brushing a strand of hair off her forehead and back into place, her eyes narrowed. "Is it Bob and this new owner you're expecting to get into a fight?"

"Well, maybe not a fight," said Giz, "but they don't want to miss whatever might happen. There's not much for them to do these days. Austin, Nevada's not what it used to be."

Kimberly nodded absentmindedly, as she gathered her mail into a neat bundle. She started for the front door, then paused. Turning slowly with her arms folded, she returned to the counter.

"Morgan told me Bob wanted that ranch, but that was nearly a year ago. And he's been trying to buy it all this time?—it's no wonder he's upset."

"How long will you be in town?" asked Matty, suddenly.

"I was going to pick up a few salt blocks, then pay some bills before heading out. Why?"

"If you wait a few minutes, you can meet Jason," answered Matty. "He usually comes in about this time every Saturday to pick up supplies."

Kimberly sighed. "I suppose it would be a good idea to meet him," she said, then glanced at her watch and again headed for the door. "I'll go do some errands. If he's here when I get back, you can introduce us, otherwise I need to get back to the ranch."

As soon as Kimberly had gone, Matty Gibson looked over her shoulder. After making certain no one was near and after sending Giz to the storeroom, she went outside to the town's payphone and cunningly picked it up. "I want to report some cattle rustling," she whispered hoarsely. "There's a tractor-trailer rig out on Gold Venture Road loading up with steers—and they're doing it through a cut fence. Get the sheriff out there, quick!"

Hanging up quietly, she went back inside and sat down in the swivel chair, then slowly leaned back with a mischievous curve to her lips. A few moments later, as Kimberly passed by the front window, Matty Gibson watched a white Blazer and squad car roar down Main Street, heading west. Coming to her feet, she rushed to the door. Opening it, she craned her neck to see around Kimberly. "That looks important," she offered innocently.

"Must be," replied Kimberly, watching the truck speed by and disappear down the grade that led out of town. "Bob doesn't take a backup, unless it's serious."

Hoping to buy some time, Matty stalled. "Wonder what it could be? Maybe you ought to stay and find out."

"No. I can't. And I'm sure Bob will tell me all about it when he hears I'm back. I really don't have the time to—"

The door to the rear of the store slammed loudly, interrupting Kimberly's train of thought. Both women turned to see Giz walking up the main isle with a customer.

Powerfully built, and noticeably taller than Giz's five foot ten inches, he immediately caught Kimberly's attention—and held it. Even in the dimly lit store, and with fifty feet between them, she noticed his gray-blue eyes contrasted sharply with his tanned skin and dark brown hair.

"I told you he was a looker," said Matty under her breath. As the two men grew nearer, she added, "You two would have some beautiful children!"

"Matty!" gasped Kimberly, her eyes glaring wide with shock. "What has gotten into you?"

Quickly walking to the glass counter, Kimberly turned away from the approaching men and began sifting though her mail. She pretended not to notice them, but as they grew nearer, her face flushed with color.

"Kimberly Lynn Whitney," whispered Matty in amazement, "You're blushing! I never thought I'd see the day!"

Expressively, demandingly, Kimberly cleared her throat, as she continued shuffling.

"Look who came in the back way and already loaded up his own supplies," announced Giz with a grin. "Said he didn't want to get in anybody's way."

Scowling at her husband, Matty raised an eyebrow, then nodded at the man next to him. "I just saw 'anybody' heading out of town, Jason. I think he'll be gone for a couple of hours or so."

"What makes you think so?" asked Giz.

"Heard there was some rustling out near the Robertson place. That's a good two hour round trip."

Suddenly suspicious, Giz glared at his wife. "How'd you know—?"

"Jason," blurted Matty quickly, "I would like for you to meet someone." Placing a hand on Kimberly's shoulder, she gave a slight tug and turned the young woman around. "This is Kimberly Whitney. She's your neighbor, just to the south of you. She owns the Rocking CW."

For a brief moment, their eyes met, then each politely glanced away as Kimberly formally extended her hand. "Glad to meet you, Jason. And your last name?"

Jason hesitated, then uncomfortably took her hand. "Nice to meet you," he returned, in a soft but strong voice, as their eyes again met. "I had no idea you would be—"

At the sudden loss of words, he awkwardly let her hand go.

"That I would be a woman?" offered Kimberly sternly.

Seemingly confused and obviously disturbed, Jason shook his head slowly and averted his eyes. "No. No—I knew that already," he said, then spun on his heels and abruptly left the store.

Kimberly glanced at Matty with dubious surprise. "Did you say 'polite'?"

Fred and Digger appeared from behind a freestanding shelf of veterinary supplies and hurried over to Giz. "What happened?" asked Fred, anxiously scratching the back of his neck and staring at the back door.

"I don't know," shrugged Giz. "Something come over him—and he just left."

Unsatisfied, Digger asked, "What did?"

"Beats me," replied Giz. "But like I said, I've seen 'em like that before. You never know what's inside their head."

As the rest of the old-timers again began to congregate, Matty motioned for Kimberly to follow her out the front door. "Let's go have a cup of coffee. There's something I want you to know about Jason."

"I should be going, Matty. Whatever it is you want to tell me about him is really not my concern."

"That may be, Kimberly," said Matty kindly. "What just happened surprised me, too, but I think maybe I know what caused it. You might have accidentally been responsible."

"Me!" exclaimed Kimberly, as Matty maneuvered her out the door and down the sidewalk. "What could I have possibly done?"

The two women walked past several empty lots and vacant stone buildings until they came to the International Hotel. Built in 1863, it was the oldest hotel in Nevada and the city of Austin's only attraction. It served strong coffee and was a good place to eat. It was also the only place to eat.

A pair of men wearing greasy baseball caps looked up as the door squeaked open, but otherwise the large dining room was empty. Crossing over the faded carpet and ignoring the lustful stares, Matty and Kimberly took a corner booth with a window looking out onto the main highway.

The board and bat wall adjacent to them, and the one opposite, was cluttered with rusted mining tools, old bottles and a dusty collection of cheap Remington reproductions. In the middle of the dining area, several tables sat empty, surrounded by metal frame chairs. To the rear was a seldom-visited gift shop.

"Well, I'm listening," said Kimberly, as she glanced out the window. A lone brown pickup was parked across the street. It didn't belong to anyone she knew, and that included almost everyone in the county. Leaning back into the seat, she crossed her arms and waited.

Matty leaned closer to the tabletop between them. "Like I told you," she began in a low tone, "normally, he doesn't say much to anyone, and some people say he's unfriendly. But that's just not true. I think it's more likely he doesn't care to have any friends."

"Sounds like the same thing to me," replied Kimberly sarcastically. "And from what I saw, he needn't worry about having any."

"Give him a chance now," insisted Matty. "He's just not ready to deal with people, yet. I think he believes the less they know about him, the more likely he'll be left alone."

A stocky waitress with dark red hair and bawdy makeup poked her head out of the kitchen into the dining room. "Be with you in a second," she called across the room.

"Just two coffees, Doris," returned Matty, pointing to herself and Kimberly.

Picking up two brown mugs and a coffee pot, the middle-aged woman crossed the floor with quick short steps and set them down. With her heavily painted lips curled into a friendly smile, she asked, "How are things in Colorado, Kimberly?"

"Just fine. How are things around here?"

"Oh, the usual," sighed Doris. But after pouring the coffee, she spotted the brown pickup parked outside. "But there's a new man in town," she added excitedly. "And you talk about a looker! And the shoulders on him!"

Kimberly rolled her eyes and took a sip of coffee. "I believe I just met him. His name is Jason?"

"Yeah. What do you think?" replied Doris, as she flicked her eyebrows up and down. "Quite a hunk, eh?"

"He looked—nice. I didn't have a chance to form any opinion."

"Well, stick around, honey. That's his old Jeep pickup over there across the highway, and he usually comes in on Saturdays before he leaves town."

Mildly irritated with her predicament, Kimberly frowned at the waitress as she turned and started for the kitchen. After adding some cream to her cup, she stirred her coffee and glanced impatiently at a clock on the wall.

"Well, anyway," resumed Matty seriously, "he had been here for about a month, coming and going without saying much to anybody, when one day, he came to pick up a load of posts. They weren't in yet, but Giz was due back with them directly, so I asked him to wait a while, so he wouldn't waste his trip to town.

"I gave him a chair, and I hope to tell you—he sat in that chair nearly an hour, without moving or saying a word. Finally, I went over, thinking to start up a conversation. But when I got closer, I could tell something was really wrong. He looked different, somehow.

"Anyway, I asked him how he liked Nevada, and he looked up at me—" Matty paused for a moment as her eyes saddened, and she somberly shook her head. "And Kimberly, if you could have seen his face when he looked up… Then he said to me that it wasn't like he thought it would be—that he had come to start a new life, but couldn't forget the old one."

Kimberly's expression softened as she studied Matty's face. "What was he trying to forget?"

Matty swallowed hard, but had not yet touched her coffee. "As it turned out, this particular day was the one year anniversary of his wife's death."

Kimberly slowly unfolded her arms. "Her death?"

"But that wasn't the half of it," continued Matty. "It must have been awful for him, afterwards. Just terrible!"

"Afterwards?"

Holding her coffee cup with both hands, Matty stared into it. "He was a paramedic in San Francisco. His wife was in law school and working part-time for an attorney there, too. On that day, the year before, he was called out on an evening rush hour traffic accident.

"A drunk had run a stoplight and plowed into a small compact car. The person in the car was trapped in the twisted metal. Even though she was screaming in pain when he got there, Jason could only work on the drunk while the fire department tried to free her. The drunk lived, and the woman died."

Kimberly's face paled as her eyes opened wide. "And the other woman was—his wife?"

"He didn't know until he got back to the fire station. When he told me, I was so lost as to what to say, I just stammered like a fool. I was surprised he confided in me and shocked by what all he told me."

Reaching out, Kimberly laid her hand on Matty's. "It would have been awkward for anyone."

"Right or wrong," sighed Matty, "I said it was time he started to get out more and not be alone so much."

"That's sound advice, Matty. It's nothing to be ashamed of. A year's long enough. Life has to go on."

"That's basically what I told him. But when I suggested he was young and should think about marrying again—he stopped talking. I mean, he turned back in that chair and sat there, staring at nothing, just like he was before. I don't think he took offense to what I said so much as he just withdrew. Kind of sunk down inside himself."

Shifting uncomfortably, Kimberly leaned back and took a second look at the Jeep. Although dented and scratched, it was clean, and obviously well cared for. "I'm glad you told me this," she said, turning her attention back to Matty, "but I'm still not sure what it has to do with me."

Curiously, Matty looked at Kimberly. "Don't you see? Something about you disturbed him deeply. People talk a lot about him, like they do anybody new, but no one has ever claimed he was rude. He's always been polite to the point of being formal."

"I'm sorry, Matty. I still fail to see what you're driving at."

Suddenly, the tension breaking, Matty laughed aloud. "Girl, you've been running a ranch too long! You should pass by a mirror, sometime. You're a beautiful woman."

Kimberly wrinkled her brow, then shook her head.

"Well, even if you don't see it, Jason did, and he wasn't ready for it. I think he even felt guilty about seeing it—and that's why he acted as he did."

For a moment, Kimberly did not reply, but her face warmed with color as a ghost of a smile brightened her face. "I really should be getting back home," she said, starting to rise. "If you see Bob, you might tell him I'm back."

"I'll do no such—"

The squeak of the café door ended Matty's boisterous refusal and sent Kimberly sliding back into her seat and closer to the window. Boot heels, muffled by the thin carpet, echoed the slow, even steps of someone approaching. "Excuse me."

Surprised by Kimberly's sudden actions, only now did Matty look up. "Jason," she exclaimed, in a high-pitched voice. "What can we do for you?"

With his eyes focused on the napkin holder at the far end of the table, Jason spoke softly. "I wanted to apologize to Ms. Whitney. Despite the way I acted, it was a pleasure to have met you. I'm sorry if I offended you."

After an uneasy silence, Jason took a step backwards. "Thank you," he said, then, after a short pause, turned to leave.

Matty opened her mouth to speak, but thinking better of it, glanced at Kimberly. A second later, Kimberly responded.

"I accept your apology," she said formally, then, with more genuine feeling, added, "Would you care to join us for coffee?"

Jason stiffened at the invitation, then looked out the window at his truck. He wanted to go, to just get in his Jeep and drive. But he had already made a bad impression on the woman, and she had accepted his apology.

"Coffee for you, Jason?" encouraged Doris, from behind the counter.

"Ah—yes, please," he answered finally, then reluctantly grasped a nearby chair and set it down at the end of the table.

After pouring his coffee, Doris scampered back to the kitchen, only to reemerge and rest her fleshy white forearms on the countertop, straining her ears to hear what was being said.

Thankful he had something to occupy his hands, Jason took a sip of coffee and stole a quick glance at Kimberly. She was beautiful—disturbingly beautiful.

"Since we are to be neighbors," she began smoothly, "we might want to discuss a few things—if you plan to run cattle, that is."

"That's what I'm here for."

"I assume you have the same range allotment Mr. Morgan had."

"Yes. It was part of the sale of the ranch. I believe that is customary here."

Matty moved, as if to leave. "Perhaps I should let you two talk business and get back to the store. Giz will be looking for me."

Kimberly flashed a wide-eyed scowl at Matty as a muffled chuckle sounded from the waitress behind them. "I can't stay long, either," said Kimberly hastily. "I've been away from the ranch for nearly two weeks."

Feeling a wave of embarrassment that was fringed with a surprising amount of irritation, Jason Burkhart suddenly glanced at Matty, then looked squarely at Kimberly. It had been more than a year since he had experienced anything but grief, yet now his skin was growing hot, and his eyes flickered with intensity. "When it's more convenient then," he said flatly, scooting his chair away from the table.

Kimberly winced at Matty, as if asking what to do next, then slowly turned to Jason. But the man sitting next to her somehow looked different. His blue eyes seemed brighter, and his face was more vibrant. Yet—there was something else—something she could only feel.

"Are you free tomorrow night?" asked Kimberly impulsively, hoping to salvage Jason's feelings. "Matty and Giz are coming for dinner. I would like you there, too, if you can come. There are things we should discuss."

Hiding her surprise at the impromptu invitation, Matty forced a smile. "Please do, Jason. We would enjoy your company, and Maria is an excellent cook."

For a moment, Jason studied the two women. This wasn't going as he had planned. Just make an apology—that was all he wanted to do. Now he was trapped. Still feeling strangely irritated, he answered reticently, "It would be a pleasure."

Explosively, and without warning, the café's front door swung open, slamming against the wall, as a tall and powerfully built man in a sheriff's uniform charged into the room. "All right, you," he snarled, pointing at Jason, "on your feet!"

Jason did not turn to see who was coming towards him, nor did he stand. The voice was all too familiar. Until now, the man had merely been a tolerable nuisance.

"What is it this time, Sheriff?" he asked, calmly pushing his mug further into the center of the table.

"You know good and well—" blustered the sheriff, then caught sight of Kimberly and Matty. "Kimberly," he stammered in a subdued tone, "you're back!"

"Yes, Bob. Just got in. I was going to call you tonight."

Nodding his head, his eyes shifted from her to Jason, then narrowed with accusation. "Is he trying to move in on you, too?"

Putting his calloused hands on his knees, Jason said, "Excuse me, Ms. Whitney, Matty." Then, coming to his feet, he stood face to face with the sheriff. Looking up more than two inches into reflective sunglasses, Jason Burkhart remained cool, but for the first time in three months, it was a struggle to maintain control. "Maybe we should conduct our business somewhere else, Sheriff."

A taunting smile spread across the big man's face as he slowly removed his glasses, revealing a one-inch scar above his left eye.

"Getting brave, are we?" mocked the sheriff. "I do my job wherever and whenever I want. And right here, and right now, I'm putting you under arrest."

"For what?" asked Burkhart, his skin again growing hot under his faded cotton shirt.

"For calling in a false criminal report. I was halfway out to Gold Venture Road before it dawned on me—it was just your way of trying to sneak into town. Those cattle out that way were shipped last week."

Acting surprised, Matty interrupted. "I don't think Jason would do such a thing as that, Bob." Then, thinking quickly, she asked, "How long ago was it that you got that call?"

"A couple of minutes before I left town," answered the sheriff confidently. Still facing Jason, he continued, "I was standing right there in the office when it came in."

"Well then, it couldn't have been him," replied Matty. "I was talking to him at the store when you went down the highway, and had been for at least ten minutes before that."

Smoothly, and with only a wisp of a smile, Jason turned to Matty. "Thank you, Mrs. Gibson," he said courteously, then once again faced the sheriff, who stood blocking his way. "If there's nothing more, I'll be going."

For a slow count of ten, the two antagonists stood inches apart, as the sheriff glared threateningly into a pair of expressionless, unblinking eyes. But as he had done since the hazing began, Jason Burkhart chose to ignore the harassment. Stepping to his right, he started for the door, but when he reached it, the bigger man snickered insultingly.

Pulling the door wide open, Burkhart paused and looked back at the officer. With their view blocked by the booth, neither Matty nor Kimberly saw the silent but blistering message written in Burkhart's glare.

For months, the sheriff had waited for the day his quarry would tire of the chase and anxiously anticipated the moment he would see him squirm under pressure and finally lose his composure. Yet, what he was seeing now was far from what he expected. As the door slammed shut behind Burkhart, and the big man took a seat next to Kimberly, his eyes flared with uncertainty.

Matty glanced at the sheriff. He was noticeably pale around the cheekbones, and his perpetual arrogance had evaporated. "You know, Bob," she said, watching him closely, "Giz was saying just this morning that he thinks everybody has misjudged Jason—that he might not be one to push too hard. Maybe you should go a little easier on him."

Bob Muller's head snapped up. "What do you mean?" he asked defiantly, but his tone was laced with doubt. "He's nobody! Just another gutless blacktopper from California. The sooner he leaves the better."

Matty suppressed a smile. "What makes you think he's leaving?"

"You know as well as I do they never make it out here. They come here for the—the 'pristine desert'—then the heat and hard work knocks the hell out of them, and they tuck tail and run back to their cities and suburbs."

"Well," said Matty, as she got up from the table, "we all can't be fourth generation Nevadans. He's been working awfully hard on that ranch, and he doesn't look very worn out to me." She paused for effect, then added, "Does he, Kimberly?"

As Matty stepped out onto the sidewalk, Doris picked up a pot of coffee and held it high. "Sheriff?"

"Yeah, Doris, and a piece of pie with it." Then, staring straight ahead, Muller said, "I suppose you had business with that guy."

"Yes, I did," answered Kimberly, casually. "I guess you know he bought the Morgan place."

Muller's jaw muscles rippled under his smooth shaven skin, and his lips grew tight and thin. He glanced at Kimberly from the corner of his eyes. "That's old news."

"We got only apple today," announced Doris from halfway across the floor. Setting the pie plate and cup down noisily, she poured the coffee. "You know, he's really not a bad sort. You ought to give him a little slack, Sheriff."

"Well, now," snapped Muller. "Isn't he Mr. Popular today!"

Allowing the sheriff time to cool down, Kimberly took a sip of coffee and found herself looking out the window, searching for the brown pickup truck. Seeing it was gone, she set her mug down. As Bob Muller forked a piece of pie into his mouth, she looked out the window again. "How did you know he was from California?"

Hastily swallowing the piece of pie, Muller washed it down with a gulp of steaming coffee. "I stopped him a few times. He hasn't got his Nevada license, yet. When he showed up driving that old truck, I just naturally had to stop him for safety checks. We got to know each other real well."

Kimberly frowned disapprovingly. “There’re a lot of old trucks in town that look worse than his. What else do you know about him?”

Suddenly losing his appetite, Muller abruptly pushed the plate away. Knocking the crumbs from his lips with the back of his huge hand, he studied Kimberly closely. “I know his last name is Burkhart, and that he’s not wanted for anything. At least, I haven’t found anything yet.”

“What do you mean, ‘wanted’?”

“Oh, it’s the way he acts.” answered Muller thoughtfully. “About the third time I pulled him over, it came to me how much he reminded me of an ex-con or a parolee, so I called in on him. But there was nothing. He was clean.”

Trying to seem disinterested, Kimberly asked mildly, “What made you think he was a criminal?”

The sheriff shrugged, “Because he’s always acted like a con. No matter what happened, he never got mad—or at least he never showed it. He wouldn’t hardly say a word except ‘yes’ and ‘no.’ And he’s never looked me in the eye for more than a second or two.” Muller paused thoughtfully. His eyes narrowing into slits, then he added, “At least—up until today, he didn’t.”

“Is that all?”

Sheriff Muller chewed on the inside of his cheek for a moment, anger spreading across his face. “Kimberly, there’s some things about this you don’t understand,” he said tensely. “It would be best if you just stay out of it. He’s got the look of a man that’s done some hard time, and acts like one, too. I’ve seen enough to know.”

“But you said he was clean.”

“Yeah,” replied Muller with a dark grin. “But I’m not through with him, yet.”

“Bob, I don’t want anyone to get hurt over this. Whatever is between you two, it’s not worth jeopardizing your job.”

Bob Muller's grin grew larger, until a row of white teeth showed behind his pale lips. "There's only one person around here in jeopardy, and it sure as hell's not me!"

CHAPTER TWO

A pair of linen curtains billowed gracefully in the predawn twilight as they caught a tepid gust of wind then settled gently back into place. On the floor of the small ranch house, a black and tan hound licked at the air twice, then swallowed lazily before going back to sleep. In the wood frame bed, Jason Burkhart lay on his side, staring out the open window at the fading darkness. Only half-aware of the monotonous ticking of a battered alarm clock, he watched until the last star disappeared into the morning sky.

It had been a long and restless night, but surprisingly, he felt rested. Reaching for the clock, he flipped the alarm lever to OFF, and checked the time. He had never liked waking to clattering bells or buzzers and habitually arose a few minutes before they sounded. Still, each night, he set the alarm to go off, just the same.

Dressing in faded jeans and a long sleeved cotton shirt, Burkhart shoved his feet into battered western boots, and then paused to scratch the top of the dog's head. "How are you this morning, Trouble?" he said, wiping the sleep from his eyes. "Looks like it's going to be a good day. Especially for a no-good, lazy dog like you."

Yawning widely, the hound came to its feet, then bowed and leaned into an arching backwards stretch before following his master into the kitchen. Next to the stove, on a worn out piece of linoleum, he flopped down and curled up again.

Lighting a flame under a blue-speckled coffee pot, Burkhart took two cans of chili con carne from the shelf above him. When he had some eggs frying in a skillet, he opened the cans, tore off the labels, and set them on the last two burners. With weeks of practice, his timing had become precise, and as if on queue, the coffee steamed, the chili bubbled, and the eggs baked solid white. A minute later, Burkhart sat alone at a small table eating in silence, watching the sky grow blue and occasionally sipping steaming coffee from a thick porcelain mug.

When the sun broke the horizon, he finished his third cup and stepped into the outer room. Taking his flat brimmed hat from a deer antler nailed to the wall, he tucked a pair of worn leather gloves under his belt. "You coming?" he asked, turning back towards the hound and opening the door. "Let's get going."

The air was still cool, and a remnant of the earlier breeze still rustled the sagebrush, but the rays of the newly risen sun seared whatever they touched. As Burkhart opened the truck door, the dog hopped onto the seat, panting excitedly.

Fighting a wagging tail, Burkhart shoved Trouble to the passenger's side of the Jeep, then started the engine. In the bed were thirty creosoted posts, a six-foot steel rod, and a clamshell post-hole digger. Strapped to the side of the bed was a red five-gallon gas can and a large water jug with a metal cup wired to its base. As the engine warmed, Burkhart rubbed his dog behind the ears, while his eyes moved over the last two month's work.

The century-old board and bat house had been painted and re-roofed, and the barn, which had been near collapse, was now squared up and reinforced with new beams. Most of the boards in the corral and loading chutes had been replaced, and the cattle squeeze was now welded into working order.

Beyond the barn lay two hundred acres of what once was permanent pasture, and for the last week, Burkhart had worked twelve hours a day building a new fence around it.

Yet even with working long hours in primitive living conditions, Burkhart seemed to thrive in the desert elements. He relished the demands of each day and took deep satisfaction in the accomplishments of a hard day's work. With planning, ingenuity, and pure brute force, he had done much to restore the ranch to its former order—and the string of endless chores kept him from thinking too much.

He had always been unusually strong, but working the ranch was better than any gym. He had gained nearly ten pounds, most of it in his chest and arms. And with his shirts growing too tight, he was glad to have some new ones from the hardware store to wear that evening at Whitney's ranch house.

At first, he was irritated with himself for accepting the dinner invitation, and in fact, wondered why he even bothered going to the restaurant and apologizing to her. He had made things worse by interrupting her when she was talking with Matty—and then there was the incident with the sheriff. None of it had gone well. He should have minded his own business in the first place. But this morning—this morning, things didn't seem quite as bad as yesterday.

Shifting into gear, Burkhart started down the dirt road towards the unfinished fence, then braked suddenly, sending Trouble onto the floor of the cab and scrambling for his feet. "She forgot to tell me what time to come!" he protested, with half-hearted indignation. Then, feeling an unexpected sense of relief, he sighed heavily, as if a burden had been lifted.

It had been over a year since he had socialized with anyone for any reason, and his new life was one of undisturbed simplicity. Only after moving to the ranch, had he realized any vestige of tranquility since his wife's death. He sought the desert to be left alone, to retreat and shield himself from any more grief. Up until now, he had succeeded. He was in control. Each day was predictable and peaceful.

"I just won't go, then," he said, then smiled thoughtfully. "Can't be expected to show up, if I don't know the time." But as he drove on, he realized his relief was tainted with a nagging regret. And with the regret came the bitter taste of guilt.

By noon, fifteen posts had been set thirty inches into the rocky sand. Hand packed with the forty-pound rod, they stood strait and rigid along the fence line. With his shirt soaked with sweat and dust, Burkhart tossed his gloves on the lowered tailgate and drained the jug of its last cup of water. As he wiped his neck with a handkerchief, Trouble growled deeply. Crawling out from under the shade of the Jeep, the hound stared in the direction of the house, which was slightly lower in elevation than the truck, close to a mile in the distance.

Coming in on the dirt road, and still a quarter mile away from the house, was a pickup. Judging from the light dust trail, it was moving slowly.

Burkhart nursed the last of his water, watching the truck drive up to the house. With nothing of any value inside, he was in no hurry to go down and investigate. He wanted no visitors, and he hadn't invited anyone to the ranch.

A lone figure appeared at the rear of the house and headed towards the barn. Halfway there, the person stopped, then turned around. A moment later, instead of leaving, the truck made its way up the fence line, coming straight for him.

Frowning, he laid the cup down on the rear fender. Lifting his sweat stained hat, and using his fingers as a comb, he brushed a wet lock of thick brown hair from his forehead, then set the hat back into place. Bristling and barking fiercely, Trouble trotted out to meet the intruder as the sun glared off the windshield, masking the identity of the driver.

"That's enough, Trouble," growled Burkhart, as the dog reluctantly stopped barking, but kept pace with the truck until it came to a complete stop.

"Is it alright to get out?" asked a feminine voice.

Burkhart slowly came to his feet, squinting in disbelief. "He won't bite," he replied, vainly pulling the clinging shirt from his sweaty chest.

The door swung open, and Kimberly Whitney stepped out. Smiling at Trouble, she knelt down on one knee and put her hand out. "Come here, fella," she said in a soft and genuinely friendly tone.

The dog, as if suddenly embarrassed, sheepishly dropped his head. Wagging his tail with exaggerated effort, he shyly waddled up to her.

"Good boy," praised Kimberly, giving him a pat on the head. "What kind is he?"

"Until now, he was a vicious watchdog," said Burkhart disgustedly.

Kimberly laughed. "I'm sure he's a good watchdog. He just knows who to trust, that's all." Coming to her feet, she reached back inside the truck for a cream-colored western straw hat.

With hat in hand, she took a few steps forward, then paused to look behind her. In the brightness of the midday sun her light brown hair, now pulled back into a ponytail, showed streaks of blond. "You do nice work," she said, after glancing down the fence line.

Burkhart self-consciously brushed sand from his pants, gazing at the loose white blouse and form fitting blue jeans in front of him.

"Well, I don't know. I think it will hold up," he said, now looking into eyes that somehow seemed even more beautiful than the day before.

"I was sitting in church this morning and suddenly realized I hadn't told you what time to come for dinner tonight. So I thought I'd come over and tell you to be there around eight—if that's alright."

"Eight?" replied Jason, uncomfortably. "That's—that would be fine."

"You know where the turn off to the ranch is?"

Burkhart nodded, but then said, "You know—I don't want to cause you any trouble."

Tugging her hat into place, Kimberly's shaded eyes darted over Burkhart's partially unbuttoned shirt and the powerful chest that pulled it tight. Somewhat distracted, she took another step forward. "What do you mean?"

"Pardon me, and I know this is none of my business," began Burkhart slowly, "but I gather you and the sheriff are—together. He won't like it that you and I—that you are having me over for dinner. Even if it's business related."

Kimberly stiffened noticeably, then her brown eyes ignited and burned into him. "You haven't been here long, Jason Burkhart, so I'll excuse you for being so forward. I assure you, I do business when, where, and how I choose, and nobody tells me who I can and cannot see!"

Burkhart blinked in surprise. Wondering how she knew his last name and at her angry response, he smiled admiringly. "Does the sheriff know that?"

Kimberly's eyes flashed at the question. "Dinner is at eight," she said flatly, then turned on her heels, walked back to the truck, and drove away in a cloud of dust.

Watching the pickup disappear, Burkhart jerked the hat off his head and threw it against a fence post. "Why the hell did I say that!" he roared into the empty desert. Disgusted, he shook his head and mumbled, "I can't believe I did that!"

As Burkhart finally set the last post of the day, the uneven desert terrain was streaked by long shadows and the colors, bleached out by the day's heat, were beginning to return. Glancing at the sun, he realized the last several hours had passed more quickly than he thought, and for the first time in nearly a year, he wished he had worn a watch.

Hurriedly, he packed the truck and opened the cab door. "Load up, Trouble," he said irritably, "We're going to be late."

Roaring and bouncing down the fence line, they were back at the house in less than three minutes, and Burkhart sprinted into the bedroom. "I knew it!" he said heatedly, scowling at the battered clock, "Seven-thirty."

Quickly filling a ten-gallon galvanized tub with water, he took it from the kitchen to the front porch. Stripping down, he tossed his clothes in a pile, and with a bar of soap, stepped shin-deep into the water. After wetting himself thoroughly, he scrubbed frantically until he was lathered from head to toe, then stepped out of the tub back onto the porch. Grabbing the two metal handles, Burkhart jerked the tub of water over his head and turned it upside down.

Soaking wet, but clean enough, he hurried to the bedroom, snatching a towel as he passed through the kitchen, and his denim jacket off a chair. In a matter of minutes, he was dressed, and using a small round shaving mirror as his guide, combed his hair the best he could.

Racing to the Jeep, he remembered the sign off the highway that pointed the way to the Rocking CW and calculated his time. If the main house was not too far from the turn-off, he could still make it without being late. "Out, dog!" he said to Trouble, who sat expectantly behind the steering wheel. "You're not invited."

The hound hopped down, then turned a sullen face towards Burkhart, who rolled his eyes. "You'll live—now stay here and keep an eye on things." Driving away from the house, Burkhart checked the dog in his rearview mirror. "It'd probably be best," he muttered, "if we traded places. I think everybody would be happier."

An even mile from the highway turnoff, Burkhart pulled up in front of the Whitney residence and knew he had made it in time. A station wagon, nearly as old as his pickup, was parked next to a white pickup with the ranch brand painted on the door. He stopped alongside it and turned the engine off. What he saw then made him wish he had taken more time to get ready, or at least worn better clothes.

A walkway made of flat stones, and lined with red and yellow flowers, led through a neatly kept lawn to a magnificent two-story house. Easily a hundred years old, it was in perfect condition, and judging by its size, must have had at least a dozen rooms. As Burkhart reached the front door, his heart began to pound heavily. He hesitated, then with rock-hard knuckles, tapped lightly and took a step back.

A short, plump Mexican woman in her sixties opened the door and cast an appraising glance at Burkhart. Then, with an approving smile and a mild Spanish accent she offered, "You must be Mr. Jason. Come in, please."

"Jason is just fine, ma'am," said Burkhart politely. "No 'Mr.,' if you don't mind."

"I'm Maria, Jason. I am happy to be meeting you," she replied, then extended her arm. "They are this way, please."

Following Maria down a long hallway covered with several generations of people in black and white photographs, Burkhart entered a large open room with a high ceiling and red tile floor. In the center of the floor was a long, heavy wooden table, neatly set, and beyond it a massive fireplace made of stone. To the right was a pair of French doors that led out into a garden, and to the left, a second set of doors opened into another part of the house.

"I'll tell them you are here," said Maria, before going into the adjacent room, and from the sound of it, out a third door. In a moment, Giz and Matty appeared, each holding a half-full glass of iced tea and sporting a pair of quizzical grins. "Good evening, Jason," offered Matty, crossing the spacious room with Giz in tow.

As Giz extended a meaty hand, Burkhart glanced past him, hardly feeling the vigorous handshake. With silky, sun-lightened hair draped behind bare shoulders, Kimberly entered the room wearing a full-length, white Mexican style dress that fit snugly around her small waist.

"Hope you brought along a big appetite," said Giz heartily. "They set a good table out here."

"Sure," replied Burkhart, unable to force his eyes from Kimberly.

"It's been a while since breakfast."

"It's not wise to skip lunch," offered Kimberly with an expressionless, but strikingly beautiful face.

"Ordinarily I don't. But today—I forgot."

Kimberly raised her eyebrows, as if surprised. "A busy day?" she quipped, coming alongside Giz.

"No more than normal. It just—time got away from me. It was a better day than most."

A faint smile brightened Kimberly's demeanor and softened her eyes. "Then it is time to eat. Jason, you may sit next to Matty over there," she said, pointing to the opposite side of the table, "and Giz and I will sit here."

With the two ends of the long table empty, they sat in the middle, Giz across from Matty, and Jason across from Kimberly. Seconds later, Maria brought out two long candles in crystal holders, placed them on the table, and lit them. "You are ready?" she asked.

"Yes, Maria," answered Kimberly, then added wryly, "and thank you so much for the candles."

Maria winked at Matty and smiled knowingly. "You are welcome, Miss Kimberly. It is not often that they are called for at this house."

Returning with a cart of steaming hot food, Maria set the dishes down in the center of the table as she announced each one proudly, "Enchiladas, chili rellanos, tacos, tortillas, rice, and ribs."

Giz chuckled and scratched his jaw. "Ribs?"

"In case Jason does not care for Mexican food," explained Kimberly.

"Not everyone has the same tastes."

Jason smiled and shrugged. "That's very considerate," he said, then looked up at Maria. "But nothing can beat good Mexican food."

Maria beamed with delight, as she sat down a pitcher of milk. "Gracias, Senior."

"De nada," replied Burkhart, with a nod.

Matty cocked her head curiously. "Do you speak Spanish, too, Jason?"

"Some. It's hard to live in California and not pick up some of it. It's a beautiful language."

The dinner was scattered with polite conversation, and it was not until coffee was served that Kimberly mentioned the subject of ranching. "How long will it be before your fence work is done, Jason?" she asked.

Burkhart's brow wrinkled, and for a moment, he seemed distant. "I guess I never gave it much thought," he answered, surprised at his own words.

"I see," answered Kimberly, glancing at Matty for her reaction. "May I ask what type of operation you'll run?"

"Cow-calf."

"And how will you start up? How are you going to stock your range?"

"Well," began Burkhart deliberately, "I planned on getting one hundred bred-back heifers or good cow-calf pairs. A hundred steer calves, to get some money coming in, and three or four bulls."

Giz leaned back in his chair and let out a long whistle. "I hope you got a good banker behind you. You're talking about a big piece of change there."

Burkhart did not reply, but looked uncomfortably at Kimberly, who, like the others, dubiously waited for his response. Finally, forcing himself to speak, he said softly, "There was an accident—and there was insurance—life insurance. And I sold everything we owned, as well. I have no need of a bank."

Giz was stunned into silence, but his mouth dropped open, and his face flushed with embarrassment. Matty lowered her head and rubbed her brow, but Kimberly gazed deeply into the steady blue eyes across from her. "I'm very sorry to hear that, Jason. I am sure it was a terrible loss."

Burkhart nodded imperceptibly, then took a sip of coffee. "I admit I don't know much about cattle," he offered, easing the tension and changing the subject, "but I think I can learn enough to make do."

Kimberly's eyes narrowed with concern. "You mean you haven't run cattle before—of any kind?"

"You're taking a mighty big risk, Jason," warned Giz. "The cattle business is tricky, at its best. There's not a lot net profit per head. A lot of things can go wrong and put you under in a hurry."

"I know, Giz. I've read enough to at least know what the problems are, and I realize I need experience. I'm flying down to New Mexico soon, on a tour of five of the top ranches in the state. I'll get some ideas there."

Folding her hands and leaning her elbows on the table, Kimberly smiled half-heartedly. "You're going to have a tiger by the tail, Jason. But I'll say one thing for you. You're on the right track."

"Oh?"

"I went on that tour a few years ago. You can learn a great deal in a short time, and much of what they do there works well here, too."

"When do you leave?" asked Matty.

"Well, actually, tomorrow morning. I'm catching a flight out of Fallon."

"Will you be gone long?"

"Three or four days, at least, but I can't stay much longer than that."

Kimberly seemed deep in thought, and then said, suddenly, "You do understand that our allotments are adjacent to each other, and that the land is open range out there?"

Burkhart nodded.

"We have a cow-calf operation, too, and our cattle are going to wander onto each other's land. It usually helps if both parties work together during the gather and branding. Does that sound okay to you?"

Uncertain how to respond, Burkhart blinked. "I—but your ranch is so much larger. I don't see that I could be of much help to you. Seems like you'd be getting the short end of that arrangement."

"Well, consider this. I have good stock. If you buy your calves from me this year, it will save me shipping costs, plus you'll donate some of your labor bringing them in. And I have a supply of bred-back heifers you may want to look at, as well."

Laughing aloud, Giz said, "Now you can see why Kimberly here is one of the best ranchers in Nevada. She's got a head for business and knows how to make a profit."

"Sounds like a good offer, Jason," encouraged Matty. "It's kind of the way things are done out here. We try to help each other. It's too hard to stand alone and make it."

Burkhart shrugged. "It's fine with me. And I would be happy to buy all my cattle from you," he agreed, then added shrewdly, "and it'll save me shipping costs, too."

"You learn fast," said Kimberly. "Welcome to the ranching business. Now, who wants dessert?"

Before Giz could accept, Matty smiled graciously and cut him off.

"Thank you so much, Kimberly, but we really must be going."

Checking his watch, Giz protested, "But it's only nine o'clock!"

"Yes dear, but don't you remember? We have such an early start tomorrow, and I'm sure these two have a lot to talk about that doesn't concern us."

Squinting sideways at his wife, Giz studied her suspiciously.

"Give Maria our compliments," continued Matty, as she slid her chair back and moved around the table towards Giz. "And, Jason, you have a good trip."

Reluctantly, Giz pushed his large frame away from the table.

"Thanks for the feed, Kimberly. Nice to have you back." He then reached out to shake hands with Burkhart. "Next time I'm out, I'll have to come by and see what you've done with all those posts I sold you."

"You're welcome anytime," replied Jason, realizing he meant what he said.

As the two abruptly left, Kimberly watched in amazement, and then slowly turned back to Jason. "Well—would you care for dessert?"

Caught off guard, unexpectedly alone with Kimberly Whitney, Burkhart felt as if a bee had been let loose in the pit of his stomach. "Sorry. No room."

"They are gone so early?" questioned Maria, as she returned to the dining room with more coffee. "Must be something important for Mr. Gibson to leave without at least one piece of pie!"

"Apparently so," agreed Kimberly, still puzzled by the early departure.

Maria glanced at Burkhart, and then caught a glimpse of Kimberly. Even in the soft glow of candlelight, she seemed to be blushing. "It's a nice evening, Miss Kimberly," she said, circling behind the table to the French doors. Pulling them open wide, she inhaled deeply. "It is nice in the garden, too. Many of your father's roses are in bloom."

"Roses?" questioned Jason skeptically, "Out here in this desert?"

"It is only a desert now," answered Kimberly. "Once it was very green, and before that, it was the bottom of a huge lake. The soil here will grow most anything. All it needs is water."

"I never thought of it that way, but I'm sure you're right. Only, flowers seem so delicate, and this country is so rough and unforgiving."

Kimberly tipped her head towards the open doors. "Shall we take a look?"

Burkhart paused as the sweet fragrance of roses drifted in from the garden, and allowed himself a moment to appreciate the glory of candle light caressing a young woman's face. "It would be a pleasure."

Kimberly met him as the two rounded the end of the table, then, walking side by side out the French doors, she formally put her arm through his. Overhead, a quarter moon cast blue shadows on a grassy lawn while highlighting the roses with a gray-white glow. A soft breeze stirred the warm night air, and from an open window came an occasional clatter of dishes being washed.

The garden was completely enclosed by a six-foot, adobe brick wall, and the roses grew all around its base, except for a break in front of a narrow gate. "There are several different varieties," said Kimberly, as they stepped to the right and started around the yard. "But I won't bore you with names."

Jason Burkhart smiled thoughtfully. "Nothing seems to be very predictable in this desert. So many unusual combinations."

"Combinations of roses?"

"No," answered Jason, gazing at the moon. "Of the desert and cattle, for one thing. Who would have thought this would someday be cattle country? Or for another, pickups and pretty women. Of—a night out here—the smell of roses in the air—and me—on a walk with you."

Gently coming to a stop, Kimberly turned towards Jason, her expression hidden by the shadows. "Is that such an unusual combination?"

Jason raised an eyebrow. "Until this very moment, I would have thought it impossible. Two days ago, it wouldn't have entered my mind."

With her arm still in his, they walked slowly on, then Kimberly offered, "I want to apologize for the way I acted this afternoon. I'm afraid I was quite rude."

"I took no offense. It was none of my business to ask what I did."

"No." replied Kimberly firmly. "You were just being considerate."

"Was I?" asked Jason, reaching out to touch the petals of a small rose. "I'm not sure that was my motive."

"Bob and I have known each other since childhood. People make more of our friendship than they should."

"And the sheriff? What does he make of it?"

"I've always been honest with him. We grew up together, shared good times and bad. We have a great deal in common, and we're very good friends but I'm not in love with him."

As they came to the gate, Jason asked, "Where does that go?"

"Out into the desert. I often walk there in the evening."

"Alone?"

"My mother passed away when I was very young, so I used to go with my father. He taught me about this country and life, like his father taught him. He's been gone several years now, but he gave me an appreciation for the simple things—showed me beauty where others saw only emptiness."

Jason shook his head. "It was the emptiness that drew me out here. I felt at home with it."

Kimberly thought for a moment, then let go of Jason's arm and stepped towards the gate. Using both hands, she lifted the cast-iron latch and shoved on the heavy beams. With a metallic squeak, the door to the desert swung wide open, allowing in a faint gust of wind.

Once again taking Jason's arm, but this time more snugly, Kimberly smiled sympathetically. "Serenity can heal the soul," she said, then with a gentle tug started for the desert.

Following her lead, Jason looked down at the hand that lay across his arm. “True. But it takes more than that to bring the spirit back.”

For several minutes, they walked across the sand in silence, both feeling the warmth of the other as the darkness cooled the night air. Several times, they glanced at one another with an unspoken awkwardness, but there was no attempt to separate.

Finally, they came upon a small bench encircled by a ring of stones and stopped. “My father and I used to sit there,” said Kimberly. “I was ten years old when I put the rocks here. It was our special place.”

Jason looked at Kimberly from the corner of his eye. “I’m sure it still is.”

Kimberly glanced up, trying to read his expression in the dim light. “My father and I were very close, but after mother died, he was never quite the same. He was the same good person, but never as happy as when she was alive. Even at thirteen, I could see it. I asked him once if he had ever considered marrying again. He just smiled, put his arm around me, and said, ‘Kimberly, if I went looking for someone to take your mother’s place, I’d never find her. No one could do that. Doesn’t work for me or anybody else.’ But then he held me a little closer, and said, ‘but having lost someone you love is no reason to never love again.’”

Jason turned to face Kimberly. Staring hard into her moonlit eyes, he started to speak, but was cut short.

“Matty told me,” offered Kimberly. “She told me about your wife, Jason, and I’m very sorry about what happened. I hope you don’t mind her telling me. She thought I should know.”

Pausing for a reply, she looked at him earnestly, but in the darkness could only sense the tension.

A moment later, Jason took a deep breath and exhaled slowly, as the stiffness drained from his body. “Maybe she’s right,” he said thoughtfully, his eyes drifting into the shadows.

"Father never met anyone else he could love," continued Kimberly in a soft, reassuring voice, "but he was here most of the time and had little opportunity. I would hate to see someone like you waste away out here where there are so few people. Before you become too involved, perhaps you should reconsider the ranching prospects and think more about yourself. Not just of a day to day existence—but the years ahead."

Jason reached up slowly, took the hand from his arm, and held it gently, its very touch stirring the relentless emptiness that had buried his heart. "I wish I could have known your father," he said. "It would have taken someone special to raise a daughter like you."

Kimberly's face flushed. "I—you do understand what I'm trying to say?"

"Yes I do. And I appreciate the advice. But I don't believe I'm able to use it right now."

"Why not?"

Jason sighed painfully. Then reluctantly, with confusion in his voice, he replied, "When I saw you yesterday, when I first looked into your eyes, I felt something. I was almost—almost drawn to you. But I've regretted feeling that way ever since. I couldn't sleep last night for thinking about it. There was a sadness, almost a fear of something slipping away—the feeling of someone letting go—I really don't know what it was."

Surprised by the intimate words, and unsure of their meaning, Kimberly hesitated for a moment, then said compassionately, "Jason, I'm sorry for what you're going through."

There was a long pause, then in a less confident tone, she added, "But I'm glad you felt about me as you did." Rising up on her tiptoes, she kissed him softly on the cheek. "Shall we call it a night?"

Jason let go of Kimberly's hand and gazed deeply into her eyes. Then with a faint smile, he extended his arm. As she took it again, he said, "Your father was a wise man."

CHAPTER THREE

Maria yawned, rubbed the sleep from her eyes, and walked slowly down the hallway. It was a half-hour before daybreak and time to start breakfast, but when she opened the kitchen door, the lights were on. Coffee was perking, yet the scent of flowers filled the room.

Kimberly looked up from the kitchen table. With her eyes narrowed in thought, she merely nodded her hello. In front of her was a fruit jar, and in it, a dozen roses of varying shades of red and yellow. Next to the flowers was a faded jeans jacket.

Blinking her eyes to clear them, Maria said, "You are up early this morning, already dressed—And picking roses?"

"Just a few," answered Kimberly. "I didn't sleep very well."

"Are you feeling alright? Do you want me to get you something?"

"Oh, no—I was just thinking of Dad."

Picking up two coffee cups, Maria sighed. "He did love his roses," she said, then filled both cups and sat down beside Kimberly. For several moments, they drank their coffee in silence.

After glancing at a wall clock, Kimberly began rearranging the roses. "I was so young when mom passed away. I really never knew what he went through—what he was feeling. What was it like Maria? How long was he hurting?"

Maria stopped drinking her coffee and stared at the flowers. "I don't know, Kimberly. A long time. I remember thinking to myself, how long would it be before he smiled again—no, actually laughed again.

"Except for you, there was no joy, no happiness in anything. He just worked. Oh, he worked so much. But I could see the emptiness in his eyes—and I don't think it ever came back—not like when your mother was here."

Pulling a red rose from the jar, Kimberly gently brushed it across her cheek. "Dad told me once, when we were walking in the rose garden, that a person could love again after losing someone. Do you think Dad could have? If he hadn't been out here alone so much—and if he had met someone new, I mean. Do you think it's possible to do that, Maria?"

Again sipping her coffee, Maria looked at Kimberly from the corners of her eyes. She looked once more at the roses, then at the jacket. "Mr. Whitney was a good husband and a good father," she said sincerely. "He was a successful rancher, even during the hard times. He had many friends and was respected by everyone. All this can only be said of a wise man. If Mr. Whitney said a person could love someone again, it is because he knew it to be so. And he could only have known that if he felt it in his own heart."

Kimberly studied the rose in her hand as if it were a puzzle, turning it slowly with her fingers. "It is odd when you think about it."

"What is?"

"Roses—in the desert. He thought it was so strange."

Maria put her cup down. "Who?"

Suddenly clearing her throat, Kimberly laid the flower on top of the jacket. "I think I'll get an early start this morning."

Going to the stove, Maria picked up a frying pan. "Do you want breakfast?"

"No, thanks. I had some toast. And I may go into town later."

"You'll get hungry before noon, if you don't eat. You're too skinny. You'll get light-headed, you know?"

"Yes, Maria. You've been telling me since kindergarten."

Taking her coffee cup to the sink, Kimberly opened the cupboard door beneath it and looked in the trash. "Do we still have those rib-bones from last night?"

"What do you want with them?"

Cocking her head to one side, Kimberly merely sighed.

Maria shrugged and pointed. "There on the top in that white bag. But I don't know why you should want them."

Kimberly took the sack, then grabbed the single rose and jacket. Offering no explanation, she walked out the back door.

An annoying buzzer sounded, waking Jason Burkhart from a deep sleep. Reacting instantly, he slammed his hand down on the top of the clock, then slowly sat up. Scratching his head and yawning, he tried to remember the last time he heard the alarm. It had been close to a year, at least.

Reaching down he gave Trouble a pat on the head. "Slept in this morning," he said, then slipped on his jeans and shirt. "Guess it doesn't make any difference, since all I have to do is pack a few things for New Mexico. So we don't work this morning—as if you ever did any, anyway."

Sitting down on the bed, he pulled on his boots and looked out the window into the fading darkness. The ranch was remote, with rolling hills to the south; it was totally isolated. There was nothing to see from where he sat, but a few miles across the vast Nevada desert, in a magnificent house, was his only neighbor. And last night—last night, she had offered to help him with his cattle. They would share a fence line, they would work together on occasion, and perhaps he would see her in town sometime. What was a young woman like her doing out in the desert? She was a capable woman and owned and operated a large cattle ranch, but somehow she remained completely feminine. So many women that assumed jobs that traditionally belonged to men became man-like. Why that was had always puzzled him, but now he had met an exception to the rule.

Turning his attention back inside, Burkhart shook his head to clear it. When he reached for the peg where his jacket should have been, he jerked his hand back as if he had been stung. "Crap!" he blurted, then repeated more forcefully, "Crrr—rap!"

Disgustedly, he looked again at the hound that lay half-asleep at his feet. "She's going to think I'm pretty stupid. Can't even manage to take care of my own clothes—much less a cattle ranch!"

Trouble raised his head off the floor and yawned. Jason scowled at him. "And what is it with you and her anyway? Some watchdog you turned out to be. The first visitor we get, and you suddenly get—what was it—bashful or scared? A complete stranger—and you act like the two of you were old friends. Just worthless!"

Going to the kitchen, he jerked a can of chili from the shelf, but suddenly realized he had no appetite. Holding the can in his hand, he looked at his clock. It was two hours before he had to leave, and it would only take a few minutes to gather his things for the flight.

"You know what, Trouble? For once, I'm just going to sit on the porch, drink my coffee, and watch the sunrise. Then, if I feel like it, I'll eat. For a while—just a little while, I'm going to do absolutely nothing."

Setting the can down, he thoughtfully rubbed the side of his face. She had kissed him—on the cheek—but still. Gazing down at the hound that now sat at his feet, Burkhart's brow wrinkled with uncertainty. After a long pause, he muttered softly, "Crap."

Kimberly Whitney turned off the engine of her truck. She hadn't used her lights since turning onto the gravel road that led to the old Morgan place. The small ranch house was still two miles off in the morning twilight, but when the window lit up she saw it easily.

Kimberly picked at a callous in the palm of her hand, then looked at herself again in the rearview mirror. For the third time, she pushed an unruly lock of hair behind her ear. What would he think of her dropping by so early? But then again, it wasn't considered early in this part of the country. Everyone tried to avoid working in the hottest part of the day, but did he know that yet—that it wasn't really that early? Looking at the jacket next to her, and then at the ribs, she began to feel foolish. On impulse, she reached for the ignition, then drew her hand back. No. He would want his jacket, and he should have someone look in on his house and dog. He would never ask anyone—he didn't even know anyone, and she was his nearest neighbor. Of course, it wasn't out of the ordinary.

Sitting back in her seat, Kimberly looked at her watch. The eastern sky was bright, but the sun had not crested the horizon. When it did—then she would drive the rest of the way.

Rolling down her window, she welcomed the cool desert air on her face. A slight gust of wind brought with it the fragrance of sage and the fluttering sound of unseen wings.

What was it she was feeling? What had kept her awake throughout the night? Was it pity for Jason Burkhart, a sentiment somehow linked to the memories of her father and mother? Or was it more? She had asked the same questions all night, and without any answers, she had ended up here—waiting—but for what?

Across the valley floor, ten miles to the west, the mountaintops now blazed with yellow-orange, and Kimberly started the pickup down the narrow road. He would have been up for up for ten or fifteen minutes by now, but she drove slowly, just to be sure.

When she was two hundred yards from the house, Trouble darted out of the sage, barking and nipping at her rear tire.

Knowing that Jason would now have some warning of her arrival, she felt a wave of relief. Poking her head out the window, she smiled. "Good boy, Trouble," she said heartily. "Good boy!"

At the sound of her voice, the hound slid to a stop and quit barking. A second later, he caught up to the truck, wagging his tail and looking up at Kimberly as he trotted alongside.

Kimberly stopped a few feet in front of the front porch, then put her hand out the window before opening the door. The hound reared on its hind legs to take a sniff, then reared again and licked her fingers.

Catching sight of Jason in her peripheral vision, she reached inside the sack and took out a bone. Disguising her uneasiness, she opened the door and let the dog snatch it from her, then watched it scamper off. When it was completely out of sight, she stepped out of her truck.

Turning casually towards the house, Kimberly glanced up. Jason stood quietly at the edge of the porch, looking at her as the yellow rays of morning brightened his face and illuminated the blue in his eyes. Her legs suddenly felt heavy. Her heart started to race, and for a moment, she forgot why she had come. But in that same instant, she knew that what she had been experiencing, what had kept her up all night—was not pity.

"I hope I didn't wake you," she said, coolly. "But I wanted to catch you before you left. I brought your jacket."

Jason Burkhart knew he should respond, but he only stared at the young woman in front of him. A desert sun rose behind her, and the air was still. There was perfect silence, and for a few seconds, enshrined in the light, she did not move. It was a vision most men only dreamed of, a rare glimpse of almost unimaginable beauty—and he wanted to remember it.

Forcing himself to speak, he said, “Thanks. It was dumb of me to leave it. Sorry.”

Maintaining her composure, Kimberly continued. “I also wanted to offer to look in on your place while you were away. You know, check the horses’ water, and see how Trouble is doing. I should’ve talked to you about it last night. If I had, I wouldn’t have to bother you this morning.”

“Oh, I’m not bothered at all. I was just having coffee and watching the daybreak. You want some? I have plenty.”

Kimberly nodded. “Sure.”

As Jason left to get another cup, she reached inside the truck cab for the jacket, then froze. She didn’t remember having done it, but the jacket lay neatly folded with the red rose slipped inside a buttonhole. “Kimberly Lee Whitney,” she muttered. “Get hold of yourself.”

After removing the rose, she grabbed the jacket and spun around, only to find Jason waiting with her coffee. “Did you say something?” he asked.

“Not really,” she answered, as she exchanged the coat for the cup. “Just talking to myself.”

After blowing on the steaming coffee, she carefully took a sip, then went to the porch steps and sat down. Looking out into the desert, with Jason standing behind her, she spoke easily, “You make your coffee strong. I like it that way, too.”

The increasing warmth stirred the air, and the rising sun changed the drab desert sagebrush into a brilliant blue-green blanket. In the distance, a lone quail began to call. “I had a good time last night,” said Jason. “I didn’t think I would, at first. But it turned out alright.”

“Why did you think that?”

"Well, it seems like ever since we met, all I've done was get you upset. And you invited me over anyway. I thought that maybe it was something you felt you had to do—because I moved in next to you. It could have been you really didn't want me there, or something like that."

Kimberly shrugged her shoulders. "Well, actually, you weren't too far off. But I think the way the evening ended was nice."

Glancing down at Kimberly, Jason noticed that she sat to one side of the step. He again brushed the side of his face where she had kissed him. It was, of course, only out of sympathy—a sign of compassion from a very understanding woman. "Yes, it was a good night. And thank you for the advice. I also wanted to apologize again, for yesterday, when you were here. What I said about you and the sheriff was none of my business. I don't know why I did that."

Taking in a deep breath, Kimberly let it out slowly. "I love the mornings here in the desert," she said wistfully, "and the sunsets, too. But I like the mornings the most, because everything is starting over. It's always the beginning of something new—even if it's just a little something. Let's just forget yesterday."

Jason smiled and took a sip of coffee. "I rise on the wings of dawn."

"You can quote from Psalms?" asked Kimberly, pleasantly surprised.

Chuckling softly, Jason scratched the back of his neck. "So now you know I'm not a complete heathen. Tell me something about you that I don't know."

Kimberly laughed. "Okay, I'll tell you a big secret that only you and you alone will know."

"What would that be?"

"I don't bite."

Understanding her meaning, Jason awkwardly took a step forward. "After yesterday afternoon, I wasn't sure," he muttered, then sat down next to her. For an instant, their shoulders touched, then quickly separated, yet the distance between them was less than two inches.

Trying to sound serious, Jason said, “Maybe you don’t bite, but you bark pretty good.”

“Do not,” replied Kimberly, then playfully elbowed him in the ribs.

For the first time in a long, long while, Jason Burkhart laughed. And in that laughter, with him beside her, Kimberly suddenly found encouragement. At least he was able to laugh again.

Sitting together, neither spoke for a full minute, but the silence was a comfortable one. Kimberly glanced at Jason and smiled to herself. Though there was a slight space between them, she felt his closeness. It was a sensation as perceptible as the sun’s rays on her skin, yet the radiance it generated was like nothing she had ever experienced.

“You’ve done a lot with the ranch,” she said, finally. “Old Morgan would be proud of you.”

“It keeps me busy, and it helps me sleep at night.”

“Yes, there’s plenty of work on a ranch,” agreed Kimberly, then unable to resist, she added, “but last night, for some reason, it was my turn to lose sleep. In fact, I didn’t sleep, at all. I finally gave up and got up two hours early.”

Jason looked at her curiously. “That’s strange. I overslept this morning. I never do that—at least I haven’t for a long time.”

Hearing the comment, Kimberly felt her heart jump, but calmly drank her coffee.

“Sounds like Maria’s cooking agreed with you,” she said, but hoped that wasn’t the real reason. “She could open her own restaurant, if she wanted.”

For a moment, Jason thought about it. “Yeah. That could be it,” he replied honestly. “But what’s your excuse?”

It was an opening, but Kimberly balked. It was premature—or was it? He was going to leave in a few minutes, and she would not see him for days. It would give him time to think of her, to at least consider her as more than just a neighbor. And she desperately wanted to say something—anything.

Setting her cup down, she clasped her hands around her knees. "Do you really want to know? Truthfully?"

Jason set his cup down, as well. "My dad taught me it was always the best way to live your life. Maybe not the easiest way, but the best way. Go ahead. It was likely me, and all the problems I caused you, but go on—I can take it."

Unclasping her fingers, Kimberly stood up. "Can we walk up to your loading pens? I'd like to take a look at them."

"Sure," answered Jason, then came to his feet. "It's that bad, huh?"

"No. Hopefully not."

Thinking of what she would say, Kimberly walked up the dusty road, with Jason by her side. Seeing a small stone, she kicked it with the toe of her boot and watched it roll into the sage. "Truthfully?" she repeated.

Squinting his eyes, Jason rubbed the back of his neck and rolled his head. "Why does it suddenly feel like I'm going to the dentist?"

"It's not that bad!"

"Well, the suspense is getting to me."

With her eyes straight ahead, Kimberly took a deep breath. The morning had been so beautiful. "When you're in New Mexico, I want you to think about something. The reason I didn't sleep last night—the reason was that I was thinking of you—not about the ranching and what we talked about last night, but in a—more of a—romantic way."

Jason Burkhart stopped walking. He was stunned, and his face showed it. At that moment, Kimberly turned and glanced at him. Then she panicked.

"I'm sorry Jason—I—I'm so sorry! I shouldn't have said anything. I feel so—"

Jason's hand came up quickly, his fingertips gently silencing her lips. Their eyes met and held. Taking his hand away, he gazed at her in wonder. He struggled to speak, but no words came. There was too much he didn't understand, too much to explain. Taking her by the shoulders, he leaned forward, looked into her eyes, and then softly kissed her.

Jason drew back, and for a moment, Kimberly's eyes stayed closed. Then, slowly, they opened. She started to speak, but he pulled her to him and kissed her again.

"When I get back," he said, looking again into her eyes. "When we have more time, I would like to see you again."

Kimberly's heart was pounding, yet she had never known such serenity. "Then I will wait until then. And Jason, your father—was also a wise man."

CHAPTER FOUR

A faded blue sedan slid around the last bend in the deserted road, blasting a turbulent wall of dust and gravel into the heat waves, then fishtailed wildly before regaining control. It was the last ranch on the Land of Enchantment tour, and Jason Burkhart was late, very late.

Just ahead was a massive log gate frame, with the letters MT painted across the top beam, and Burkhart slowed his rented car until the dust trail faded out. To do otherwise in any rural area was to invite trouble, and he was already pushing his luck by arriving late. Passing under the heavy beam, Burkhart turned left into a makeshift parking lot, where two acres of dried yellow grass was filled with sport utility vehicles and pickup trucks.

Pulling into a likely spot in the rear, he got out and quickly looked around. Opposite the lot was a vacant stockyard divided into several pens and an array of gates and chutes. Beyond that was a cluster of white clap-board buildings; with no one in sight, he made his way to the largest structure in the group. As he started up the front steps, a screen door opened.

"Your name Burkhart?" asked an elderly man with white hair and a gray handlebar mustache.

"Yes it is. Looks like I'm too late."

"Sure are," replied the man, half standing in the doorway, holding the screen open. "They left nearly an hour ago. Said you might be along."

"Any way I can catch up to them?" asked Burkhart hopefully.

"Not likely. Don't know exactly where they was goin' first. It's a big ranch."

"Great!" mumbled Burkhart, wiping the sweat from his forehead.

"Gonna be a hot one today, I reckon," said the old man. "Already ninety, and not yet ten o'clock."

"Yeah. The air conditioner on the car went out just before the flat, which was just after I took the wrong turn."

"The name's Travis McWilliams," grinned the New Mexican, who suddenly seemed much younger than Burkhart had first imagined. "There's cold water in the ice box inside. Come in and help yourself."

Entering after McWilliams, the screen door slammed shut behind Burkhart before he could stop it from banging noisily into the jam. The sound echoed into a large, barn-like room, and Burkhart took a moment to let his eyes adjust. The floor was empty, except for a small couch and coffee table just in front of a stone fireplace. Around the edge of the floor, along the walls, were additional chairs and a few reading lights. In the corner to his left was a card table, and to his right a door, which stood open.

Taking a seat on the couch and propping his right leg up on the coffee table, McWilliams motioned with his thumb, "Kitchen's in there," he said, pointing to the open door.

Realizing he must be in the living quarters of some of the ranch hands, Burkhart crossed to the door and into a small kitchen. In the second cupboard he tried, he found the glasses, then opened the refrigerator and took out a glass milk bottle filled with water.

As he filled his glass a second time and replaced the water, he heard the front door screen slam closed, and then several heavy footsteps before they stopped suddenly. With glass in hand, he returned to the outer room to see a tall but paunchy man in his late twenties looking his way.

"What's he doing in here, Mac?" he demanded, nostrils flaring.

McWilliams did not turn. Rubbing the outside of his right knee, he replied flatly, "I asked him in for a drink of water. You got a rule against that, too?"

"If he's to be hired help, he reports to me, not you. As of yesterday, McWilliams," sneered the big man, glancing at Burkhart, "you're finished as a foreman."

Assuring himself he had an audience, the man continued, "And it's high time, too. Now me and Ed can run a modern cow operation. You and his old man are history around here, and good riddance to the both of you!"

McWilliams lifted his bad leg slightly to bend his knee, then set his foot flat on the floor and stood up. With eyes full of hatred, he faced the new foreman. "Well, now, Hogan, maybe the boss would like to hear what you have to say, seeing how he's on the ranch today. Or are you just shooting your big ugly mouth off, like most cowards I've known?"

The young foreman started forward with a lunge, and then jerked to a halt, unsure of what to do next. For a tense count of ten, there was silence, then Burkhart started across the floor towards the couch.

"It seems to me, and a whole lot of other people that are here on tour, that this ranch has done real well in the past several years. Considering the state of the beef industry, that's quite a feat!"

"Nobody asked you," barked Hogan viciously. "Get out of the bunkhouse and off the property, or I'll have you arrested or throw you off, myself."

Burkhart's eyes darkened with resentment. As he moved closer to Hogan, a lethal smile spread across his face. This was just another version of Sheriff Muller, and he had had his fill of such men. "First of all, you don't have the authority to order me off the property, and secondly, even if you did, I'd advise you to call the sheriff before trying anything you would regret."

Hogan's eyes flared wide open. With his thick lips stretched tightly over clenched teeth, he lunged clumsily for Burkhart's throat.

Ducking under the grasping hands, Burkhart buried a targeted fist just below the breastbone of the charging man, bending him in two. Then, with a driving left to the cheek, and another right to an open jaw, the hulk fell to the floor, gasping for breath and bleeding.

"I think I've about worn out my welcome," commented Burkhart, as he casually turned to McWilliams. "You have any place to go? To work, I mean?"

"Nope," replied Mac, twisting the end of his mustache and studying the pile on the floor with satisfaction.

"I'm new in the business," said Burkhart, "but I've got a small ranch started in Nevada. I could use a man with experience."

"Turning out to be a better day than ever I thought," laughed McWilliams. "I'm packed and ready, Boss. You got a deal. Be back and ready to go in five minutes."

"Make it three," said Burkhart, "he won't stay down long, and if he gets up, he'll be a lot smarter the second time around. I'll bring the car over here."

Uninterested in a second confrontation with Hogan, and making certain no one else was in the area, Burkhart stepped quickly off the porch and across the empty yard toward the parked cars. As he pulled up to the steps, McWilliams was standing ready and tossed a small suitcase through an open rear window. Grabbing a saddle with one hand, he deftly opened the back door with the other, and shoved it in, as well. With a small box under one arm, he hobbled quickly to the passenger side and slid in.

"That's it?" asked Burkhart, surprised at how little McWilliams had loaded.

"You're lookin' at it," he answered, as he jerked the door closed. "That's all that matters anyway. And you can call me Mac, or Travis. Don't matter which."

"Is there any place you need to go, first? Anyone to say goodbye to?"

"No," sighed Mac, with only a hint of regret. "Not no more."

Burkhart glanced at his passenger, who stared out the side window and massaged his sore knee. On his finger was a gold band, worn thin by the years.

"I checked out of the motel this morning," said Burkhart, as he turned onto the gravel road and picked up speed. "I can leave this car at the airport. I have some business in San Francisco that won't take long. So we'll go there first, before heading home." "Where's home?"

"Central Nevada, a few miles outside of Austin. I have a small house, a barn, some corrals, and a well that will be good for irrigation, when it's fixed. There's two hundred acres I plan to put into pasture, and the ranch has twenty thousand acres of allotment for seasonal range."

"Have any stock?"

Burkhart shrugged his shoulders. "A dog and one horse. I was planning to get more horses when I get back. Before I get the cows."

"That dog of yours a cow dog?"

"Nope," answered Burkhart uneasily. "And I have no idea where to get the horses. All I've been doing for the last two or three months is building fences and repairing the chutes and corrals."

McWilliams scratched the gray stubble on the side of his bony jaw, then grinned broadly. "Sounds like we got a lot of work to do, Boss."

"Well, Mac, I wouldn't want it any other way. Do you still want in on this deal?"

"You bet I do," answered McWilliams eagerly. "I'm too old to change jobs, and I'm too young to quit. Besides—a man without a challenge in front of hisself is goin' nowhere. He ain't building nothing. There's no satisfaction in just stayin' even all the time."

McWilliams paused and took the small case from under his arm and laid it on the seat between them, then removed his hat and wiped the sweatband with a handkerchief.

"By the way, I got a bum knee, but I can work hard just the same. So don't let that bother you none. I pull my weight. Now then, what do we do first when we get there?"

"That's kind of up to you, Mac. I may be the boss, but you are the teacher, and I'm the student. I've studied the business on paper over the last year, but I need experience and practical knowledge. The only real work I've done so far is repair the buildings and build fences. You'll have to look the place over and see if we're ready to buy our stock. I'll need to know what equipment we don't have or need to replace."

"You got a bank to do business with?"

"I have the money side of it all taken care of for now, and after we finish in San Francisco, I'll have enough to cover my expenses, as long as we keep a lid on the spending. I'm closing escrow on a house I used to own. Once that's done, there won't be any more money coming in until we make a profit off the cattle."

"How many head do you intend to buy?"

"A hundred fifty to two hundred to start up. Steer calves, heifer calves, but mostly bred-back heifers."

Mac raised an eyebrow and glanced at Burkhart. "Going to take a lot of hay for winter. We have a barn?"

"I'm told we don't need one. We can tarp it and it should keep."

Changing the subject, Burkhart took a second look at the case on the seat and noticed the lid was expertly hand-carved in wood. "That's nice work," he said, indicating the case.

Ignoring the workmanship, McWilliams frowned. "It's the boss's version of a gold watch. I spent many a year on that ranch. Most of my life. Worked my way up from digging post holes to foreman and spent forty-three years doin' it. The boss and me was good friends too—but then he had a bit of a stroke a few months back, and the doctors told him to retire, or else."

"And someone else took over?"

"Yep. His son Ed did," said McWilliams bitterly, then chuckled in disgust. "And the next thing I knew, I was fired—thanks to Hogan. He said I was obsolete—all through. After more'n forty years! Just like that, I was washed up."

"What did the father have to say about all that?" asked Burkhart, adjusting the sun visor against the glare.

Mac shook his head and stared straight ahead. "That stroke changed him, took all the fire out of him. He just thanked me and shook my hand with his eyes all watered up. Then he give me that box there and walked away. That was yesterday."

Burkhart looked more curiously at the box, finding something familiar about its shape.

"Well, it looks too big to be a gold watch."

"No," laughed McWilliams. "He at least had some style left in him. There's a matched set of Colt pistols in there—1860 percussions, with powder flask and caps, too. And some .44 lead balls. Everything you need to shoot 'em is in there."

"He always knew I admired them pistols. He had 'em ever since I met him, and we used to go out on the range and shoot jackrabbits together. They're a fine set."

"Then you're saying those are originals, not replicas?"

"They're the real McCoys, alright. When he bought 'em, he was told they was used by a Union cavalry officer back in the Civil War days."

Burkhart thought for a moment, then said encouragingly, "He must have thought a lot of you, Mac. That's about five thousand dollars worth of guns. It seems like he may have been trying to say something with the pistols that maybe he couldn't put into words."

McWilliams did not reply and another mile had gone by before he slowly reached for the case and opened it. Inset in red velvet were two nickel plated and engraved pistols with ivory grips. Both had seven and a half inch barrels, and though worn from over a century of use, both were in remarkably good condition.

Astounded by what he saw, Burkhart struggled to keep his eyes on the road. He started to speak, but catching a glimpse of McWilliams, decided against it. Glaring into the open case he held in his lap, Travis McWilliams was lost, deep in the privacy of his own world, savoring the memories of a lost friendship.

They were turning onto the main highway when McWilliam's weathered face softened with a faint smile. Closing the lid over the pistols, he looked up with triumphant eyes. "I'll have to send that old coot a thank you letter. He'll be glad to know I got a good job already. Maybe he might write back and let me know how he's doin'—if he knows where I'm at."

"I'm sure he will, Mac," said Burkhart optimistically. "I'm sure he will."

Squinting at Burkhart, McWilliams asked casually, "How'd you know how much they was worth? Most folks got no idea 'bout such things."

"I worked all through high school for a gunsmith up in Jackson, California. He could repair anything that shot lead, and with that reputation, he got a lot of older firearms to work on."

"You must've done a good bit of shootin', then?"

"Yeah. I sure did. He never let anything out of his shop unless it was in perfect working order. It was a good experience, but it's been years since I've had much chance to do any target practicing."

Mac nodded approvingly, "We'll change that when we get things settled. These old pistols are a wonder. Wait 'til you see their accuracy. One-holers they are!"

The airport traffic for flights departing New Mexico was light, and the unloading zone nearly vacant, as Burkhart got out of the car and unlocked the trunk. Reaching for a single suitcase, he opened it up and removed his denim jacket, then snapped the case closed.

"What's that for?" asked Mac in astonishment. "It must be close to a hundred out here!"

"You ever hear what Mark Twain said about the summers in San Francisco?"

"Yeah, I've heard the saying," answered McWilliams skeptically. "Coldest winter he ever spent was the summer he lived in San Francisco. But I never figured it to be true. California's the land of sunshine and beach-bums, the way I see it."

Grinning broadly, Burkhart lifted the suitcase out of the trunk. "I like a man who wants to see for himself," he said, then handing the case to him, added, "I'll return the rental, and you can get your ticket." Reaching into his pocket, he brought out a packet and several bills. "Here's my ticket and some money. We need to change my flight to the next available and get you a seat, too."

"Will do," answered Mac, dragging out his saddle and resting it on the sidewalk.

"Oh, and another thing—you'll need to talk to someone about your case there. They'll want it put in the cargo section. Maybe in my suitcase. But it doesn't have a lock, though. We'll see what we can do when I get back."

Watching Burkhart drive away to return the car, McWilliams held tightly to the pistol case. "Well," he scoffed. "I sure don't intend to let a bunch of bag jockeys lose it for me. They'll stay with me, where they'll be safe."

After returning the car, Burkhart walked quickly back to the terminal with an uneasy feeling about what he would find. As he stepped through the automatic glass doors, McWilliams was just reaching the attendant at the desk, but by the time he got there, Mac's voice was booming. "But they're more than a hundred years old! You have any idea how much these are worth?"

The attendant, a woman with a rough complexion, a square jaw, and hair in a bun, showed only indifference as she glanced from McWilliams to Burkhart. Noticing the similar western dress, she asked arrogantly, "Is he with you?"

Immediately taking a dislike to her, Burkhart ignored the question.

"What's the progress, Mac?"

"We're gettin' nowhere, real fast. She only knows two words. One is 'no,' and the other'n is 'policy.'"

"Excuse me, ma'am," began Burkhart with a polite smile, "the items we're talking about here are not only costly antiques, but are also of great sentimental value. We don't have a good way to carry these securely, and even if we did, we all know that airlines often lose luggage. Obviously, he doesn't want to take that chance. Surely, you can understand why. Is there anything you can suggest to help us out here?"

The woman's jaw muscles bulged, and her beady eyes narrowed. "There are no exceptions! You will have to follow regulations, just like everyone else."

Burkhart patiently rubbed the back of his neck and took a deep breath. "What about the captain? Don't a lot of them now carry weapons in the flight cabin? Couldn't they keep the case with them, in a safe place?"

"No," answered the woman bluntly.

"Why not?"

Smugly laying both her fleshy palms on the countertop, the attendant leaned forward slightly. "It is against policy," she repeated, with bureaucratic confidence. "Now either purchase a ticket, or step out of line."

Checking behind him and seeing no one, Burkhart turned again to the gloating face in front of him. "I want to see your supervisor. And don't tell me he's not here or unavailable, because I know better." Then, stepping closer, his eyes coiled into a dark, viper-like stare. "Now!"

At the sound of his voice, the woman's head snapped back, and her hands slid out of sight. As she turned to leave, even McWilliams was startled by the commanding tone of the order.

Mac shook his head in dismay. "Give a person with a small mind a little bit of power, and it swells their head every damn time." Then, smiling broadly, he snorted, "But I'd say you deflated that one quite a bit. You pinned her ears back, I'd say."

"For a while, maybe. Her kind never seem to change, except to get even more narrow-minded. Wherever you go, you'll always find those that have learned it's easier not to think than to work things out. That's one reason I like living in the desert. People still have to think to make a living. If they don't do their job well, they're cooked."

"Ain't it the truth," agreed McWilliams, as the door behind the desk swung open, and a short, stout man wearing a suit and tie came through it.

"Hello, I'm Mr. Torbin," he offered pleasantly. "And you are?"

"This is Mr. McWilliams, and my name is Burkhart. I believe my appearance has led your attendant to some disrespectful conclusions, and her attitude is severely lacking as well as unprofessional."

While the supervisor checked the passenger list, Mac cleared his throat and glanced shrewdly at his new boss. He could use the big words if he had to.

"Ah, yes, Mr. Burkhart," said the supervisor respectfully, "This is your return trip?"

"Yes it is. I need an earlier flight and one for my associate, Mr. McWilliams."

"Certainly. Ms. Hanson explained your predicament, and I understand your problem. Of course, you've been told about the federal regulations and our policy, but what I can do is this: I'll red tag your case, personally hand carry it to the plane's captain, and make sure it is handled by him, personally. Then I'll call ahead to San Francisco and have the supervisor there oversee its return. Would that be satisfactory?"

Burkhart turned to Mac questioningly.

"Sounds good to me," he nodded. "Thanks, I appreciate your help. Is my saddle here goin' to be a problem for you?"

Looking over the countertop at the saddle, Torbin shook his head. "Not at all. We get these all the time. We'll just tie some twine around it to hold the stirrups down, and it'll be fine." Leaning back, he continued, "We have a flight leaving in twenty minutes. You'll be on standby, but I'm sure there are seats available. If you like, you may check your baggage now and go directly to the loading area."

"Thank you," said Burkhart, as Ms. Hanson came through the door and stood next to Torbin.

"I'll take the pistols now, and Ms. Hanson can take over from here," said Torbin, then added emphatically, "Can't you, Ms. Hanson?"

"I am sure I can manage," she responded sullenly. Then, without making eye contact, she shoved the two tickets across the counter.

Ignoring the woman completely, Burkhart checked the clock before picking up the tickets and handing one to Mac. "Go on ahead, Mac. I have to make a phone call to let some people know I'm coming in early to sign papers. I'll meet you onboard."

McWilliams watched Burkhart walk away, then studied his ticket for several minutes. Finally, he took a few steps, then hesitated, to take another confused look at the ticket.

"Down the hallway and turn left," snapped an insolent female voice behind him.

Gritting his teeth, Mac winced at her insulting tone. He managed to say nothing until he was several feet away, then swore softly as he made his way down the long corridor.

Approaching the loading area, his mood changed as an attractive redheaded attendant gave him a smile. "Right this way, sir," she said, directing him through what appeared to him to be a doorframe. Before going through, McWilliams stopped and studied the setup suspiciously.

"It's a security check," assured the young woman. "If you have any metal on your person or in your pockets, please place it on the table before passing through."

Mac grinned. "I get ya. You want to know if I'm one of them terrorists."

"Well," she admitted softly, still smiling, "We don't like to admit it, but that's right. But you don't look too dangerous to me."

After laying a handful of change and a pocket knife down, he started for the doorframe, but the redhead put out her hand. "Oops. I'm sorry, but we'll have to confiscate the knife. I'm sorry. This sort of thing happens all the time. I hope it's not too valuable, and you also forgot one other thing."

"I did?"

"Your belt."

McWilliams was exasperated. "You confiscatin' that too?"

The attendant smiled sympathetically. "No. Just for the metal detector."

McWilliams looked down at the large silver buckle. Blushing slightly, he turned his back on the attendant and removed it, then tossed it on the table. "If you weren't so darn pretty, this could get down right irritatin'."

"Why, thank you for the compliment. But this has become a necessary evil. You're taking it very well."

Walking through the detector, McWilliams asked, "Does it really work? Seems like they still get things on those planes, anyways."

"We do what we can. Since 9-11, we take every precaution possible."

Retrieving his belongings, Mac grumbled, "Seems like the tail waggin' the dog to me. There ought to be a better way of handlin' those that want to hurt innocent people."

"I wish there were, sir. But until we find another way, we're stuck with this. Have a nice flight."

As McWilliams peered nervously into the plane, he could see it was nearly full, but after a few minutes of searching, he found his seat in the rear of the narrow-bodied jet. Curiously inspecting what seemed to be a severe shortage of legroom, he stooped over and looked under the seat in front of him. The sound of the jet's heavy metal door being slammed shut brought him up with a jerk.

"You alright?" It was Burkhart who spoke, standing next to him.

"Who me?" replied Mac, his voice higher than usual. "Yeah. It just strikes me as a bit tight in here. Kind of like a coffin. No wonder I never flew before!"

Burkhart smiled knowingly. "It affects a lot of people that way—the first time—but you'll get used to it after a while."

Wide-eyed and paling noticeably, Mac growled, "Not in this lifetime, I won't! It just ain't natural, that's all there is to this flyin'. Ain't natural!"

Five minutes after take-off, the 727 made its final flight adjustment and leveled off into cruising altitude. A moment later, Mac relaxed his grip on the armrests, and the color returned to his expressionless face. "Now what?"

"That's all there is until we land. We'll hit a lot of turbulence in places, but it's nothing to worry about. It'll feel just like riding in a car on a bumpy highway. You want any coffee?"

"Sounds good," answered McWilliams. Noticing an attractive flight attendant in the aisle, he started feeling more at ease. "But it still ain't natural."

The slender brunette pushed a cart next to the two men. For a moment, her eyes held admiringly on Burkhart. "Would either of you care for something to eat or drink?" she asked.

"Two coffees."

Serving the coffee, she glanced at McWilliams, then looked again at Burkhart. "If you need anything," she said, with a hint of invitation in her voice, "my name is Sally. Don't hesitate to ask."

For the next hour and a half, Burkhart reviewed the ranch layout and its financial situation, asking McWilliams about breeds, birth-weights, and calving ease. They were still deep in discussion when Sally interrupted.

"Time for a break, you two," she said, smiling. "The seatbelt light is on. We're on our descent and preparing to land in San Francisco."

"You're kiddin'!" exclaimed McWilliams.

"No. You two have been at it non-stop since take off, and I might add, it has been quite an education. I think you had this whole section entertained."

Returning her smile, Burkhart agreed, "Well then, it was educational for all of us, Sally. I'm amazed at how much there is to know. It's hard to believe that cattle raising is so complicated. It's a whole lot more than grass and water."

Staring at Jason's tanned face and piercing blue eyes, Sally asked, "Will you be staying in the city for long?"

"No. Only a day or two. I have some business I have to finish up, then we're leaving for Nevada, as soon as we can get away."

"Oh, I see," replied Sally, obviously disappointed. "Your ranch is there?"

"Yes. And with Mac here as my new foreman, we're going back to build it up into something respectable. Right now, it's just a lot of empty land that's doing nothing."

"It sounds exciting, and I wish you both luck," she said. Then placing a flirtatious hand on Burkhart's shoulder, she added, "Fly with us again sometime."

Glancing at Burkhart, McWilliams grinned. "Friendly sort, isn't she?"

"I guess," answered Burkhart, then smiled, and shook his head. "But wait until you meet our neighbor. Not only is she good-looking, she's the owner and manager of the biggest ranch in our part of the state."

McWilliams' smile faded. "Not a female?"

"Oh, yeah. She's female all right. And they don't grow them any prettier or smarter."

Rubbing his chin, McWilliams squinted at his new boss. "My age or yours?"

"Mine."

"Single?"

"Yeah. We just met, but I know she's not married. There's a local sheriff that's interested in her, but I don't think it's anything serious."

"How about you?" asked McWilliams wryly. "You interested?"

Jason Burkhart thought for a moment, then buckled his seatbelt. "Actually, I am very interested."

The landing was rougher than usual, but McWilliams, although tense, said nothing. Burkhart was impressed, but thinking back on his first impression of the man, he was not surprised. He was old school, a cowboy inside and out.

As the plane taxied toward the terminal, Burkhart put on his jacket. "I'm not sure where I'll have to go to get the pistols, but you can get our luggage, and I'll find out. I'll meet you there as soon as I can."

"Uh, where do we get our luggage?" asked Mac sheepishly.

"Just follow this crowd," he said, as they filed forward towards the exit. "They'll take you where you need to go. It's no different than following a herd of cows."

Before they had reached the main lobby, a droning voice sounded over the public address system, "Mr. Jason Burkhart, Mr. Jason Burkhart, please come to the white courtesy telephone."

"Sounds like they're on the ball," said McWilliams.

"That it does. You stay here, and we'll get our luggage later. I'll find a phone, and they'll tell me where to pick up the pistols. It shouldn't take but a few minutes."

Turning quickly, Burkhart slammed into a huge muscular body, then by reflex, took a step to the side, and caught his balance. "Excuse me," he said sincerely, then looked up four inches into a pair of impudent eyes.

"Watch where you're going, next time," snarled a young man of over two hundred and fifty pounds.

Burkhart's face flushed with heat, and the hairs on the back of his neck bristled. His eyes narrowed and locked onto the large head in front of him as his feet shifted slightly to a wider base.

McWilliams spoke suddenly, yet casually. "Leave well enough alone, son. I'm sure you got better things to do with your time."

"Like what?" scoffed the young giant. "What's it to you?"

"Like learnin' some manners, for one the thing," replied McWilliams, less diplomatically.

"Well now," returned the hulk menacingly, "an old man and a runt. You think the two of you can—"

"Conally!" barked a commanding voice to the right. "Get your ass over here, or get back on the bus!"

With a smirk, Conally slowly turned, "Lucky day for you, wimp," he said loudly, then, full of conceit, strutted away.

Burkhart watched him go before glancing around with eyes that smoldered with instant anger. "Football player," he said with disgust. "Looks like a college team, one of the Pac Ten, most likely."

"There's a bunch of big ones over there," agreed McWilliams. "And that particular one was a big 'un. Maybe too big."

Burkhart nodded. "He is big alright, and strong, too. But no matter how big they are, they all have the same weak spots. Places that break and tear as easily as any man—but thanks, Mac. I don't know what's gotten into me, lately. All of the sudden, I seem to be losing control of my temper. It doesn't seem to take very much to set me off."

"We're all entitled to a temper, Jason. You don't come across as a hot head, just somebody that don't tolerate rudeness in a man. Young people, especially those that have a lot of money or fame, seem to be gettin' ruder by the day. But give 'em enough rope, and they'll hang themselves. Fall off their high horses. They will nine times out'a ten, anyway. It don't matter if it's football, baseball, or rodeo. They're almost all the same."

Burkhart relaxed and smiled at Mac with a mixture of curiosity and respect. "Sounds like you know more than just cattle."

"I've been around a while," replied McWilliams evasively. "Rode one of those high horses myself in the rodeo circuit, once. Took me years to get over being known as a has-been."

"Well, Mr. Conally will have to wait then," said Burkhart, noticing the athletes beginning to gather in a group around their coach. I'll be back in a minute."

Passing close by the football players to a nearby phone, Burkhart ignored the glares of Conally and a few other teammates, as his name again came over the address system. Lifting the receiver, he turned toward Conally, and said clearly, "This is Burkhart," then, certain he could be overheard, added coldly, "I can pick up my pistols now?"

Conally's thick neck stiffened, and his eyes widened. An instant later, he began working himself into the center of the team and disappeared from sight.

From the phone, Burkhart went a short distance to a small office, where he inspected the pistols and signed a receipt. With the case under his arm, he opened the office door to leave, but paused and turned back.

"Be sure and express my gratitude to the airlines for their understanding and cooperation," he said. "You've been a great help."

"You're welcome," returned an employee, from behind the counter. "Anytime we can—"

The deafening concussion of a nearby explosion drowned out the next word and rattled the plate glass windows facing the parking lot. Everyone in the lobby flinched violently, as several people in the lobby screamed. The attendant quickly scrambled for his phone. "This is Davis," he gasped desperately. "We've had a crash in the parking lot right in front of me. No, I can't see anything yet, but it nearly knocked out the windows. Now I see some smoke in section F or G—"

Burkhart, with his fist still wrapped tightly around the doorknob, listened intently to the one-sided conversation as his stomach began to churn at the thought of what a crash would mean. He would have no choice but to volunteer his services as a paramedic, something he swore he would never do again.

After a long half minute, Davis sighed with relief and wiped his forehead with the back of his hand. "Are you certain?" he asked finally. "Thank you!"

With a trembling hand, he put down the phone as Burkhart straightened slowly, looking expectantly over his shoulder. "It was a car," offered Davis, with nervous laughter. "In the parking lot, a car exploded, that's all."

"Anyone hurt?"

"Hurt?" stammered the attendant, "Oh, I didn't ask—but of course it will be a few minutes before we know anything. I'm sure everything is under control," he continued, regaining his composure. "There's nothing to worry about. Thank you for your concern."

"You're welcome," replied Burkhart, then walked cautiously through the door only to come to an abrupt stop.

In front of him, stunned into paralysis, stood hundreds of once scurrying travelers, and with only the hum of abandoned escalators to break the eerie silence, a morgue-like hush chilled the stillness. What for everyone had seemed of utmost importance a few seconds earlier was now lost in visions of twisted steel, mangled bodies, and the sickening fear of loved ones lost.

"Your attention, please," echoed the speakers, then needlessly repeated, "Your attention please. There has been an explosion in the near parking area caused by an automobile fire. There is no cause for alarm. No aircraft was involved. The situation is not dangerous and will soon be under control."

The announcement triggered a flood of released emotion, as scores of nearly panicked bystanders belittled their brush with mortality and broke into nervous laughter and joking conversation. But as Burkhart started back towards McWilliams, something made him uneasy. He had seen cars explode before, and felt their blast, yet for some reason, he could not relax. Was it the force of the explosion, the likelihood of its occurrence, or only the time and place he did not like?

Warily staying close to the wall, he continued, stopping every few steps to listen, to look for anything that did not fit. At first, there was nothing, but as he passed behind the football team, he saw them coming.

Ahead of him, shoulder to shoulder, moving quickly in his direction, were three men. All had dark Mediterranean skin and black hair, and each wore a long cream-colored overcoat. But it was not their coloring nor their dress that alerted Burkhart. It was the look in their eyes—in them burned a maniacal savagery that only the worst fanatics could cultivate.

Spinning immediately, he took a step in the opposite direction, only to find another terrorist closing off his escape. Before he could make a try for the main entrance, the roar of automatic weapons thundered from every direction.

Instinctively, Burkhart hit the floor, then, hearing the terrorists ordering everyone down, he tucked the pistol case under his jacket. Without moving his head, he glanced to his left, but could see little, due to the size of the person next to him. Then, except for some distant whimpering, the lobby once again fell deathly quiet.

Burkhart heard footsteps near him as at least three men moved frantically in what seemed to be a circle around his area.

"You! You!" shouted a nearly hysterical male voice to Burkhart's right. "You two, up! Up and against the wall!"

A hard, black, military-style boot slammed into Burkhart's ribs, just missing the case. "You! Up against the wall!"

As if holding his ribs, Burkhart shifted the case higher under his armpit. Clamping his arm down to hold it in place, he got up and staggered to the wall. There, holding his head low and shifting only his eyes, he caught a glimpse of what was happening.

A fourth man had entered from the front, and as two men guarded those along the wall, the other three picked out more hostages. Even though their movements seemed erratic and uncoordinated, in a matter of seconds, they had pulled ten other men from the floor.

"Move!" demanded the fifth man, then said something in a foreign language to the others. "Move out," he repeated, jerking the barrel of his gun in the direction of gate thirty-three.

One of the young men, still lying face down, lifted his head and was instantly kicked in the temple. With a grunt, his head fell back to the floor as blood trickled from his ear, and his body went limp.

A burst of weapon fire from the rear showered the clustered hostages with fragments of white acoustic ceiling and sent them stumbling forward in a united lunge.

With their weapons at the ready, two terrorists moved out in front, clearing the way of unloading passengers, as the remaining three drove the prisoners forward in a tight group. Amid the confusion, Burkhart cautiously stole a look at those around him. With the exception of him, all were members of the football team.

Considering the first three men, how they had moved in, the position of the fourth terrorists, and how they had selected their victims, he had little doubt the athletes had been targeted. Just as certainly, Burkhart knew he had been taken by mistake.

What reason they had for taking the team members, he could only guess, but what they would do to him if they discovered their mistake was not hard to imagine. That they had likely kicked to death one person already told him they would kill without hesitation. His only hope was to remain as inconspicuous as possible, as long as possible. But, even though he was built as well as any player there, he was at least ten years older, and the last year had aged him even more. In time, too little time, he knew they would discover his presence, and then they would discover the pistols!

Grimly recalling the brutal murder of Navy diver Robert Stethem, the killing of Leon Klinghoffer on the Achille Lauro, and the beheadings in Iraq, Burkhart's blood surged hot through his veins. Instantly, his primitive instincts began to surface. With no flight possible, the desire to fight reigned supreme, and the savage within him understood what must be done. He would not hesitate. If he must die, he vowed to himself, he would die on his own terms, with the last moments of his life under his control. He would die, but he would not die alone, and he would never allow himself to be executed.

For now, however, he needed time. And, if recent patterns of the hostage-terrorist drama were any indication of what lay ahead, he might just have enough time to get ready.

After being herded under an illuminated plastic sign that naively forbade the possession of bombs or firearms on airplanes, Burkhart spotted one of the lead terrorists at the entrance of a boarding tunnel.

"Faster!" he shouted in perfect English. "Move! We have a pilot!"

Suddenly, someone behind Burkhart stumbled and fell into him, buckling his legs at the back of the knees.

Clamping his right arm tightly over the pistols, he went down, taking another in front of him as he fell.

Instantly, he pushed himself up, using his left hand, then grabbed his right forearm, as if in pain and hoped his ruse would continue to work. Pausing beside the other two men as he stood, he found himself looking into the hollow, blinking eyes of the hulking Conally.

In disbelief, Conally took a closer look at Burkhart, then glanced down at the slight bulge under his jacket. The ashen young face suddenly flushed with color, and he abruptly turned and looked away. He started to move, but a metal butt-stock smashed across his right ear, throwing him into the wall.

"Do as you are told!" ordered the assailant. "Now, move!"

Leaving a small trail of dripping blood, Conally and Burkhart caught up to the others as they were leaving the corridor and stepping into the body of a passenger jet.

"By the window," came another order, given at the point of an automatic pistol. "Everyone takes a window. One on each side of the plane, and every third row!"

Unclear as to what they were to do, the first two hostages hesitated briefly and then were violently shoved into their appointed spaces. The rest of the young men caught on and obediently began taking their seats.

Burkhart took a slight side step, assuring himself of being last in line and hopefully the closest to the rear of the plane. There, perhaps, he would be least observed and more able to maneuver. In front of him, Conally staggered down the aisle with a hand over his ear, trying to stop the bleeding. He took several steps before a gunman halted him by shoving a rifle muzzle against his chest.

"You are the biggest," he said coldly, "the strongest, too. We will show them your strength, then we will show them the strength of Allah." Raising his free hand triumphantly, he grabbed Conally by the shirt and jerked him forward. "You will be the first to die for Allah!"

With their attention on Conally, Burkhart slid uneventfully into place across the aisle from him and held his eyes forward and slightly down. If only his luck would hold, he might have a chance to carry out his resolution. But now there was another life at stake, besides his own. And that, in all likelihood, would mean even less time to get the pistols out and loaded before he needed them.

After forcing Conally into his seat, the gunmen took their positions as if part of a pre-conceived machination. One stationed himself beside the opened front exit door, while two others stood outside the cabin; the fifth was apparently inside, with the pilot.

Even though well to the rear of the plane, and least observed, Burkhart knew he could not chance any suspicious movements. In time, he thought, the guards would grow lax; there might be a distraction—anything that might give him the precious time needed to load the cylinders. Under the circumstances, he would need close to five full minutes to fill all twelve chambers with powder, the lead balls, and finally to cap them.

But even if he should have the extra time to cover the chambers with grease, he had none in the case. He could only pray that sparks from the firing bullets would not detonate the other cylinders prematurely. It was always a possibility with cap and ball pistols, but he desperately needed all twelve shots if he were to have any chance of success.

Using what time he had, Burkhart began working out his plan, paying close attention to the duties assumed by each terrorist watching anxiously for any routine that might develop. If there were to be any hope at all, timing would be critical.

CHAPTER FIVE

Assuming Burkhart was still picking up the pistols, McWilliams had waited for the initial chaos to subside, then retrieved his saddle and the two suitcases. Sitting on his own suitcase and leaning against the wall where he had last seen his boss, he watched anxiously as someone was hurried away on a stretcher. Uniformed policemen hurriedly began raising a yellow ribbon across the lobby on both sides of him. To his left, several plain-clothes officers were swarming around the area where the shots had been fired, while others seemed to be separating the football team from the rest of the passengers.

Suddenly, a megaphone crackled loudly over the melee of voices and shuffling bodies. "Quiet!" ordered the speaker authoritatively. "Quiet in the lobby! This is the San Francisco police department. We need it quiet in here!"

An uneasy hush settled over the crowd. As the megaphone was lowered, all eyes focused on the athletes. "Go ahead," said the officer solemnly.

Slowly, the coach raised a clipboard and began calling out the names of the players. One by one, the names were checked off as the students answered back, but occasionally, there was only silence. Then, after a pause, the coach continued, until forty names had been read.

"How many, Coach Shilling?" asked the policeman.

"Ten."

"We'll need their names," he said, gently taking the sheet of paper. Again raising his megaphone he ordered, "Everyone, outside the barriers. Unless you have something of utmost importance to offer, go on about your business. Those inside will have to be detained until they have been questioned." Then, seeing the camera crews setting up and the newspaper reporters filing in, he added impatiently, "All media personnel will stay behind the yellow barriers. We will release information as soon as we ascertain the extent of the crisis and the danger to the hostages."

Immediately after the announcement, reporters began shoving their way through the spectators, shouting out questions as they neared the yellow ribbon, then flooding those beyond with blinding camera lights.

Responding to the onslaught, dozens of uniformed officers lined up along the ribbon, directing the inner group away from the media personnel. Forbidding anyone to answer questions, they cleared a twenty-foot space between the reporters and the people inside the yellow tape.

Suddenly, two men in dark suits ducked under the barrier and started forward. As officers turned to intercept them, both held up shields of identification and passed through to the small cluster of athletes. The older of the two, a short square-built man in his mid-fifties, flashed his badge to the officer holding the list of hostages. "Special Agent in charge, Jack Mader, FBI," he muttered flatly. "Are you Sergeant Taber?"

"Yes, sir."

Thumbing over his shoulder to the younger and taller agent, Mader said, "Agent Bishop. What have you got so far, sergeant?"

"As best we can tell, five heavily armed terrorists of unknown nationality, abducted ten hostages and have them onboard a 727 parked out in the middle of runway three. All ten taken were from the U.C. Berkeley football team."

"Coincidence?" asked Mader skeptically.

"No, sir. It doesn't seem like it. From what we see, and from the accounts of what happened, the terrorists knew where they were going, and who they wanted to get."

Mader frowned and nodded, "You say there were five terrorists?"

"Yes, sir. All male, in their late twenties or early thirties, with dark features, and most of the time speaking with a heavy accent or in a foreign language."

"We heard on the way over there were two more."

Taber shrugged, "Somehow they were killed in an explosion in the parking lot. The bomb squad is on the way, but it looks like they accidentally tripped their own explosives. So far, we've only found pieces, fragments, but we're sure they were with the other five."

Taking the list of hostages from the sergeant, Agent Mader glanced sourly around the crowded lobby, his eyes lingering on the reporters. "Get these people questioned," he said, pointing at the passengers near him. "And get them out of here as fast as you can. Anyone with critical information keep here until I get back. Agent Bishop will be in charge until then."

Mader turned and disappeared into the mass of bystanders as Bishop and Taber instructed the other officers. In a half hour, all but a handful of people remained to be questioned and McWilliams, still sitting unobtrusively against the wall, had been all but ignored.

Finally, a plain-clothes detective approached. "Your name, sir?"

"McWilliams. Travis McWilliams."

"Mr. McWilliams, did you get a look at any of the terrorists?"

"No sir. I kept my head down the whole time."

"Are you associated with the football team in any way?"

"No."

"Thank you. You are free to go."

"If it's all the same to you officer, I'd just as soon stay put. My boss is due back, and I'm to meet him right here."

Perking up noticeably, the detective asked, "Back from where?"

"I don't know. He got a call on the phone and left down that a way, just before all hell broke loose."

"And his name?"

"Jason Burkhart."

Writing down the name in a small spiral pad, the detective thumped the eraser of his pencil against his forehead. "What did this Burkhart look like?"

McWilliams leaned forward and stretched wearily. "He's probably stuck out there behind that yeller marker. He'll be along directly."

His face stiffening, the policeman lowered his voice and spoke firmly. "Mr. McWilliams, this may be the first terrorist strike of this kind on American soil, and it has just been ascertained that eleven hostages were taken. We can only account for ten so far. Now what did he look like?"

Coming slowly to his feet, Mac said clearly, "I'd say he was close to six feet tall and weighed around one ninety, dark hair, about thirty-some years old."

"And what was he wearing?"

McWilliams scratched his head thoughtfully. "I can't remember, except for the jean jacket he had on."

"Wait here, Mr. McWilliams, and I'll see what I can find out."

Several minutes passed as the remainder of the passengers were dismissed, leaving McWilliams the conspicuous center of attention. With hundreds of reporters lined two and three deep along every foot of the flimsy tape, one would occasionally call out loudly or whistle, but McWilliams refused to respond. "Blood-suckers," he muttered bitterly to himself, "Playing right into them terrorist's hands."

Yet their questions were beginning to make him uneasy. Who were the terrorists? How many hostages were taken? Did they know they were taking athletes? Were they all athletes? How could they tell who was on the team, and who wasn't?

Although McWilliams didn't acknowledge their questions, he could not help but wonder about the answers. After the run-in with Conally, the team had, for some reason, gathered around their coach. It would have been easy to identify them as a group. But how could they know them individually, since they wore no jackets or blazers?—and where was Jason Burkhart? Hard leather heels, pounding rapidly over the linoleum floor, coming in his direction, interrupted his thoughts.

"Mr. McWilliams, I'm Agent Bishop. Would you come with me, please? I would like you to look at a video tape. You may be able to identify one of the hostages. You can leave your belongings here."

Mac swallowed hard, shoved his hat onto his head, and said, "If they got him, they bought some trouble."

As the two men walked through a heavy metal door and up a flight of stairs, McWilliams asked, "Where'd they take 'em?"

"They're on a passenger jet that's pulled out onto a runway. They have one pilot. That's all we know, right now. There's been no communication, as yet."

Entering a small room overlooking the landing strips, McWilliams was introduced to a handful of people crowded around a television screen. At first, no one spoke, as each in turn took a moment to stare at the old cowboy, from his hat down to his worn, high-heeled boots.

"Let me guess," sneered a gray-haired man sporting a goatee and a fat belly. "Number eleven is going to possess a cowboy mentality!"

McWilliams leathery face tightened at the remark, and his black eyes darted around the room, then back to the speaker. "Are you airline people rude by nature, or do you just get that way from being packed up like sardines all the time?"

Bishop chuckled softly, but the man in the goatee looked as if he had been slapped across the face.

"You'll have to excuse us," offered a tall slender man, extending a fragile-looking hand. "If you just take a look here, it might help identify one of the victims of the hijacking."

Walking slowly toward the television set, McWilliams glanced out the large viewing window and saw a single airliner several hundred yards out. Neither it, nor anything near it, was moving. Turning to the screen, he knew immediately why Burkhart had not returned. The picture was frozen and blurred, but there was no question who was in it.

"Run that back where they turn the corner, Lisa, and keep it in slow motion," said the tall man. "Mr. McWilliams, do you recognize this man?"

McWilliams watched closely as he saw the group appear, then move towards the camera, and paid particular attention when he saw Burkhart fall to the floor. "Could you run that back again?" he asked eagerly. "Where they tripped."

"You can see his face better in a few more frames," responded the young woman, with a trace of agitation.

"I'm not lookin' at his face, ma'am."

The goateed face blurted out, "Then what the hell are you—"

"Dr. Webb, please!" pleaded a bald man in horn-rimmed glasses, "Go back, Lisa, and run it again, if you would."

"That's far enough," said McWilliams, bending closer to the screen. "Now let me see that tumble again, as slow as you can do it."

His eyes narrowing to wrinkled slits, McWilliams studied, frame by frame, how Burkhart lost his balance and broke his fall. At the end of the sequence, he caught a glimpse of something else and straightened casually. "That's my boss they got, alright," he said, with a faint smile, "But they got more'n they bargained for, this time!"

"Are you sure?" asked Bishop.

"Yep. Sure on both accounts."

"What do you mean," asked Dr. Webb analytically, "on both accounts?"

"He's got two pistols under his jacket," replied McWilliams. "And he does think, and act, like a real man," he added sarcastically, as he turned to face Webb. "That's cowboy mentality to you."

"That's impossible," snapped Webb. "He just came in on a flight. You can't carry weapons on airliners."

"That so?" bristled McWilliams.

The bald man stared at the FBI agent, and then glanced at the taller man. "What do you think, Bill?"

Bill shook his head. "No way, Phil. The security in New Mexico is as good as it is here. No one can get past the detectors."

All eyes shifted to McWilliams. "Well now," he began confidently, "I suppose you'd all like to believe he ain't armed, but the fact is, there's more'n one way to skin a cat. They were carried by the captain. He just give 'em a receipt and picked 'em up after he got here."

"What's the name?" asked Phil.

"Burkhart, but the receipt has my name on it."

Looking stunned, the man called Phil took off his glasses and wiped his forehead. "Bill, check New Mexico. Lisa, call downstairs and see if anyone can corroborate this."

Bishop took a radio from his belt, and then hesitated. "I better report this to Mader. If he's armed, everything is going to change."

Phil faced McWilliams, trying to collect his thoughts, then asked respectfully, "What makes you think he is armed? We didn't see anything in the tape."

"You missed it 'cause you didn't know what to look for; hopefully, them terrorists will do the same. Back that contraption up, and I'll show you why I know."

As the video played again, McWilliams pointed with his finger, "See how he's falling there? Now watch how he rolls before he hits, and how he holds his right arm. Anybody else would'a put out their arms to break the fall, but he lands hard on his shoulder."

"Maybe he's just clumsy," scoffed Webb, as he donned a pair of half-rim eyeglasses and moved closer to the screen.

As the pictures blinked by, step by step, McWilliams continued, "His right arm don't move the whole time, and when he gets up, he uses only his left. Those guns are under that right arm!"

"It seems that the arm is injured," said Phil doubtfully.

"That boy's as strong as an ox. You'd have to hit him with a sledge hammer to hurt him that bad."

Bill quietly hung up the phone he had used to call New Mexico, but said nothing until Lisa was finished.

Hearing the end of their conversation, Phil looked up from the tape. "Well?" he asked nervously.

"He picked up the guns, Phil. They were in a case that was hand delivered by the captain to the office downstairs. He left just after the explosion, so he had them with him when he was taken.

"But there's something else, Phil," offered Bill, as he cast a patronizing look at McWilliams, "The pistols are antiques."

"What do you mean—antiques?" questioned Phil incredulously, then glared harshly at McWilliams. "What about that?"

"He means they're old guns," answered Mac flatly.

Now smiling benevolently, Phil's eyes flickered towards Dr. Webb. "And—just how old are they?"

"A hundred thirty years. Well, almost, anyways."

With a wrinkled brow, Phil artfully cleared his throat. "Thank you, Mr. McWilliams," he said, as he moved across the room to a second door. After opening it, he added kindly, "You've been a great help, but I'm sure this ordeal has made you very tired. Why don't you make yourself comfortable in our lounge? We'll likely need to ask you some more questions in a while."

"I got no place else to go," replied McWilliams, walking calmly out of the room. At the door, he stopped suddenly and turned halfway around to face them all. "Anyways, one way or the other, it'll all be over in a couple of hours."

Phil nodded patiently, "We certainly hope so. We'll let you know if we need you."

McWilliams grinned knowingly and shut the door behind him, grumbling, "Today's experts, tomorrow's fools." Then, stretching out on a long leather couch, he slid his hat down over his eyes, and took a deep breath, letting it out slowly.

"Dr. Webb," asked Lisa softly, "Why would this man take those guns with him? He must have known they were useless and would probably get him killed if they were found on him."

As if he had anticipated the question, the doctor answered without hesitation. "It is certainly no surprise to anyone that a great number of American males own handguns," he began ceremoniously. "It has long been established, in the psychoanalytical field, that the pistol symbolizes the penis. Being taken hostage would be tantamount to emasculation for those who suffer from today's rampant male ego crisis. His attachment to the pistols represents his fear of loosing his manhood." Pausing to gaze out the window, he ignored the disgusted snort from Bishop, then exhaled theatrically, "And, as the pistols are inoperable, he is likely impotent as well."

The psychoanalysis ended abruptly, with the rapid pattering of a word processor receiving information from a distant data bank as it describing each athlete in minute detail. In a matter of minutes, the computer flawlessly stamped out a physical and psychological image of each hostage. As the typing ended, Bill leaned forward eagerly, “Burkhart’s not on here, yet. The computer is still searching.”

With only the low hum of the stalled processor to fill the silence, Dr. Webb strolled over to the paper read-out, lifted it and held it at arms length. After skimming the sheet briefly, he let it drop onto the desktop. “I don’t anticipate any problems from the football players.”

“Why is that?” asked Agent Bishop suspiciously.

“They are young and impressionable,” replied Webb. “Their minds have been conditioned to follow orders and accept abusive militaristic treatment. They should pose no disruptive threat, as long as they do what they are told. That will be to our advantage, as it is important that no one offer resistance. It will allow us time to negotiate with the terrorists.”

Bishop raised a disrespectful eyebrow, and asked, “What about Burkhart? You think he’s used to militaristic abuse, too?”

“That is difficult to say without more information,” answered Webb, unaware of the question’s tone. “Behaving as he has so far, I would say there is a good chance he is quite unable to cope with stress of this nature. He’s likely to become unstable and may even panic.”

Bishop put the radio to his lips and without taking his eyes off Webb, pushed the button. “This is Agent Bishop. Tell control that one of the hostages on board is armed. The on-call psychologist believes him to be unstable. Over.”

“Of course, that is a hasty diagnosis, you understand,” replied the doctor, but then added arrogantly, “However, it is based on years of clinical experience.”

“Right,” responded Bishop, with an edge to his voice. “Is there anything on that computer, yet?”

“Nothing,” answered Lisa uneasily. “I don’t think there is enough information to identify him.”

“We need to know who we are dealing with out there,” said Bishop. “This is no time to be guessing about someone's psychological profile. How the situation is handled may depend on his calculated response. Get McWilliams back in here."

"I would hardly consider him a reliable source of information," scoffed Webb.

Phil stepped quickly to the door. "If nothing else, he can give us enough data to continue the search. Apparently, all they have is a name," he said, then swung the door open and stuck his head inside the lounge.

McWilliams lifted his hat just enough to see who had opened the door. "It over already?" he asked, then yawned with feigned boredom.

"Over? Ah, no. We need to ask you some more questions, if you don't mind."

Without reply, Mac swung his legs down, but took his time sitting up. After deliberately taking several seconds to adjust his hat, he followed Phil back into the adjoining room. "What's your question?"

"Could you tell us his full name?" asked Lisa, her fingers resting expectantly on a keyboard.

"Whose full name?" returned McWilliams, with a straight face. Catching Agent Bishop's sudden grin, he slyly tugged on his mustache to cover his own smile.

"Well—" sputtered the bewildered young woman. "Your friend, your employer."

"Jason Burkhart's all I know. Don't know how to spell it, and he never told me his middle name."

"Then do you know a place of birth, or date of birth, or even the year?"

"Nope."

"What town is he living in?"

"He's living somewhere out in the desert of Nevada. I don't recall the town. Besides, he don't live in town, anyway."

Lisa punched in the information and waited for a response.

McWilliams glanced around the room, studying each face, and then the computer. "What do you need that thing for?" he said, pointing to the processor.

Phil's face was flushed, and he began to roll up the sleeves of his neatly pressed white shirt. "We need to know who we're dealing with on board the plane. A personality profile can help us predict what actions may be taken under varying degrees of stress—how much pressure they can take before breaking down—that sort of thing. Any information you have that can help us identify your friend will allow us access to certain records vital to Dr. Webb's evaluation."

"Well, I can't think of anything that's goin' to help you run him down on that thing, but I can save you a lot of time, just the same."

"How?" asked Phil bluntly, as he loosened his tie and eased the pressure on his bulging neck veins.

"I can tell you what Burkhart's gonna do," began McWilliams, casting a serious glance to Bishop. "He'll wait just long enough to get himself ready, then he'll come out fightin'—come hell or high water."

Webb smirked loudly. "What makes you think that?"

"What makes a person think anything?" replied Mac coolly.

Taking his glasses off, Webb let them dangle from a chain around his short neck and took a step closer to McWilliams. "Let me see if I have this straight," he smiled. "You don't know his full name, or where he was born, or even when he was born. You can give us no information whatsoever about him, but you can tell us with absolute certainty what he's doing at this very moment." Inhaling noisily through blanching nostrils, Webb lowered his head slightly and replaced his glasses. "And just how long have you known this Burthart?"

"That's Burkhart," corrected McWilliams, as he reached for his pocket watch. Flipping open the lid, he checked the time. "Gettin' close to six hours already," added Mac, hiding a suppressed smile. "Where does the time go?"

Throwing up his hands in disgust, Webb spun around and went to the window. Fred fell into a nearby chair, and Bill and Lisa seemed completely stunned. Even Bishop was uncertain.

"I'm not sure what you people are supposed to be working on," said McWilliams, suddenly losing his sense of humor, "but if it's your job to figure out what to do about those people out there, I can tell you for sure the boss ain't goin' to sit still and do nothin'. If you were countin' on that, you better get your backup plan ready.

"Once in a while, you meet somebody that's all up front. Right away, you know where they stand and what they're about. You don't have to guess what they'll do next because they live by, and stand for, a code that don't change with the wind. They're the kind you want as a friend, but can't afford to have as an enemy. Those folks out there pointed a gun at 'im and are likely still holding one on 'im. When they done that, they crossed the line. It's no game now. It's life or death. May be that it's only a matter of goin' down fightin', but he sure as hell won't go with just some little whimper!"

With a sudden jerk, the door to the lobby swung wide open, and Agent Mader charged in. "What's this about a hostage with a gun?" he demanded.

"The older one they took by mistake, the eleventh man, has two pistols, but they're only antiques, sir," answered Agent Bishop formally. "They are one hundred and thirty years old."

"Are they loaded?" asked Mader impatiently.

"Loaded?" replied Bishop, dumbfounded. "How could they be? I assumed they were only collection pieces."

Mader clinched his heavy jaws. "How'd you find out he had them?"

"This is Mr. McWilliams, sir, the man's employee," said Bishop as he led Mader across the floor. "He knew about the guns."

"Were the pistols in a case?" asked Mader gruffly.

"Yep."

"Did he have a complete setup?" inquired Mader, while the others stared in disbelief. "Caps and powder?"

"And lead," answered Mac coldly. "And he knows what to do with it all, too."

Swearing under his breath, Mader rubbed the back of his bull neck and paced the floor.

"Agent Mader," began Dr. Webb incredulously, "you surely do not think these weapons are still operable?"

"Why wouldn't they be?" snapped Mader, halting suddenly.

"Their age, for one thing. Even if they might still fire, the terrorists are armed with sophisticated automatic weapons. No man in his right mind would attempt to use such crude firearms against them."

Mader stared icily at the doctor. "Maybe so, but wasn't it you that said he was unstable?"

"We hadn't yet decided that," interjected Bill timidly. "We still haven't enough data to prognosticate with any degree of accuracy."

"Alright, then," agreed Mader. "Let's get three scenarios. We'll start with the worst-case first. We'll assume this is a suicide mission, a first strike of its kind on U.S. soil, and they want to make a big impression," said Agent Mader, pacing across the small floor as he talked. "They targeted the football team because they're young and strong—they're our heroes or some such thing, and in destroying them, they show their own strength and the vulnerability of our culture. Anyway, they intend to die if their demands are not met and will take all the hostages down with them." Mader paused, slowing his steps slightly. "But we're going to assume they lost their explosives in the parking lot. All they have are grenades and automatic small arms."

Glancing in Webb's direction, he asked hastily, "How much time do we have before this guy cracks?"

"I beg your pardon?"

"Before he starts shooting, or trying to? Before he can't wait any longer?"

"But isn't it more probable that they'll discover the pistols before he has any chance to use them?"

Mader sneered. "This is a worst case scenario, Dr. Webb, and in this situation, that doesn't happen."

"In that case—paranoid with a male ego crisis, a 'worst case' if you prefer—he would at first avoid doing anything that might draw attention to him. But if our negotiations with the terrorists fail, and he feels threatened, he may panic. He will believe they will come for him first, that he will be the first to die. Once he senses eminent danger, you have no more than a few minutes—say, fifteen."

"Okay, doctor, I'll buy that. Now let's say we can stall their demands for no more than three hours." Mader stopped speaking and took a moment to check his watch, then looked outside. "It'll be near dark, and there's already some fog drifting in. We'll have to be in a position by then. Who's responsible for ground crews, trucks, ramps?"

"Me," answered Bill, flipping his hand up meekly, "but I think you should consider Mr. McWilliams' opinion before going any further."

Webb's large head snapped back in astonishment, "If you want a second opinion," returned the doctor heatedly, "you'd be well-advised to consult another psychoanalyst—not an illiterate cowboy!"

Bishop cleared his throat loudly, then said, "It's a gut feeling, sir, but I would listen to McWilliams, too. I think he knows what he's talking about."

"And you think I don't," accused Webb indignantly.

"No offense, doctor," interrupted Mader, "but let's hear his side." Turning to face McWilliams, he grunted, "So? What's your opinion? What's this guy likely to do?"

Without blinking, McWilliams responded. "He'll load as soon as he can and shoot as soon as he can. And if I understand this worst case stuff, you won't have any darkness to help you get close to that plane. An hour is all you got left if you're lucky.

"Like I was just sayin' a minute ago, he won't be intimidated, and he won't abide bein' humiliated like them terrorists like to do to everybody. He's a sensible man and a fair one, but those out there—they have declared war. Doin' nothin' is like surrenderin', and he won't do that. He's not stupid, either. He knows what they'll do if they find them guns on 'im, and he knows the longer he sits there, the more likely that is to happen. In a way of thinkin', he can do only one thing, and he'd best do it quick. It's really pretty simple."

"You mean simplistic, don't you," barked Webb.

Agent Mader thoughtfully ran his fingers through his thinning hair as he gave McWilliams a second hard look. Walking to the window, he stared out across the runway at the lone jet. "It sounds right," he grumbled to himself, then said bleakly, "That's exactly what he's going to do. That's our worst case."

Doctor Webb shoved his glasses tight against the bridge of his nose. His lips puckered into a tight circle, and his eyes flared with hostility.

Glancing sideways at Bill, Mader voiced an idea. "I need at least one sniper out there to cover the front door of the plane if it stays open. It may be all we have time for, in case this thing does blow up in our faces."

"There's a slight depression in the ground for drainage," said Phil. "It approaches that side of the jet, but it's not a ditch."

"How close could somebody get before being spotted?"

"At best, three hundred yards, but at that point, it would be a straight-on shot to the exit door."

Without turning his head, Mader ordered, "Bishop, get a man out there. Get him moving, now! If our eleventh man starts shooting, maybe we can at least take one out for him."

Instantly, Bishop was on the radio and out the door. "That'll be as close as we can get for now," continued Mader, "but I want the heavy equipment standing by. We may still have a chance to use it." Moving away from the window towards the lobby door, he pulled it open, then stopped. "One more thing. I want no word of anything, or names of anybody, to be given to the press. I want the lid kept on this. I want all video tapes confiscated for National Security. Under no circumstances do I want the identity of the eleventh man made public. We don't need another Captain Rogers or Salmon Rushdi on our hands."

The door slammed tightly shut behind Mader, but the dull roar from a sudden barrage of questions sounded through the walls and into the cramped room. Then, as abruptly as they had begun, the voices melted away into silence.

Phil glanced around the room puzzled. "Why not release his name? Who is Captain Rogers?"

Bill shrugged, then looked to Lisa quizzically.

"He was the captain of the USS Vincennes," she said thoughtfully. "Several years ago, there was a terrible catastrophe. Captain Rogers was ultimately the one responsible for shooting down an Iranian airliner with two hundred ninety people onboard. After that accident, he became a marked man. Even his wife's life was nearly taken. They were eventually forced into hiding. Agent Mader was assigned to that case. It was his first experience with terrorists. Now he's considered an expert in the field of terrorism."

"Mader can't be serious," scoffed Webb. "There is no possible way this Burthark will attack. He would get himself and everyone else killed in the process. It goes against the instinct for self-preservation. He may eventually panic, but to preemptively attack a half-dozen armed men with antiques that may not even function is preposterous. It's absurd to even consider such a scenario."

"What's so absurd?" asked Bill. "Those terrorists out there don't care about self-preservation. Why should our guy be any different? And it's Burk—hart."

"Mader's a man that understands men," answered McWilliams dryly, "and he knows you never can tell what'll happen in a gunfight. The boss'll have twelve shots in them pistols, and if he's lucky, he'll catch 'em by surprise. Right now, Mader's thinkin' of extreme cases. One thing that's crossed his mind is that Jason might pull it off and not get hisself killed in the process. Now, if that should happen, and then everybody finds out who took care of business out there, he'll be marked for death, just like that navy man was, and maybe that other fella, too. That's why he don't want no names let out to the papers."

"If he 'takes care of business,' as you say," challenged Webb, "There is no way to keep that information from the public. And, of course," he added smugly, "it goes without saying—the public has the right to know."

McWilliam's eyes blazed as he again faced off with Webb. "The public's no different than any private person. And nobody's got the right to sentence an innocent man to death, just because they want to know somethin' that's none of their damned business, anyhow." Pausing, McWilliams took two steps towards the doctor, stopping only inches away. "And if everybody keeps their mouth shut, how's anybody goin' to know who he is?"

With beads of sweat sprouting on his short forehead, Webb shrank backwards a half step, then replied hotly, "Mr. McWilliams, you have a simplistic approach to life, that, although quaint, I find quite boring. If he should start shooting inside the body of that airliner, innocent people will be injured, if not killed. Mr. Burthark would be the one responsible for such carnage and certainly would be held liable. And if charges were not immediately brought against him, I would do so myself. His prosecution would send a message to everyone that these matters are to be handled by trained professionals, without interference."

"You bein' one of them elite professionals, I suppose?" asked McWilliams acidly. "God help us if decisions in this county are being made by the likes of you. You've got no right to judge a man's actions, when his life and the lives of others are at stake. Standing here—where it's safe—it's easy for you to be brave and say what should and shouldn't be done. But if you really want to see the real world, take a hike out there and offer yourself as an extra hostage. Then see how well you follow those ivory-tower rules when you're waitin' for a lead bullet to slam into the back of your head and scatter your brains on the ground!"

Phil wedged himself between the two adversaries. "Gentleman, please! It's hard enough without the two of you bickering over something that hasn't happened yet. Let's all try and keep our heads and deal with the problem at hand!"

The brass doorknob to the lobby door snapped loudly as the door swung open with explosive force. Mader charged in, followed closely by Bishop and a third agent. All three rushed to the window.

"Give me those binoculars," ordered Mader, extending his hand backwards. "All hell is breaking lose out there. A man is out of the plane, and it may be on fire. Smoke is coming out the front exit, and someone thinks they heard gunfire."

Without taking his eyes from the window, Mader brought the binoculars up, then stood motionless, peering at the plane in silence. The radios of the two other agents crackled noisily with startled voices engaged in rapid conversation.

"We still see only one man on the pavement. He appears to be one of the terrorists. Over."

Another radio voice answered, "I see some movement inside the plane from here. Smoke is still coming out the door. It's not as much as before. Over."

"What's happening?" asked Phil, as McWilliams and Webb separated and moved to the window.

"We don't know," growled Agent Mader. "One man is down, on the pavement under the front exit door. He hasn't moved since he fell. We think he's the terrorist that kept showing himself at that spot."

"Someone's coming out!" echoed an excited, metallic radio voice.

"Turn those down!" ordered Mader. "We can see as much as they can."

There was a long pause, then he spoke again, tensely. "There's one hostage. One more. Another one. Come on! There's another one. What the hell is going on out there?" shouted Mader excitedly. "The pilot is being carried out."

Lowering the binoculars, he handed them to the third agent, took out his own radio, and turned up the volume, listening anxiously to the conversation coming in.

"We count twelve, including the pilot. No weapons in sight. Over."

"Anything visible inside?"

"When they get a hundred yards out, start moving in. But do it slowly. Over."

"Understood."

McWilliams glanced at Agent Bishop. "What's that all about?"

"They may be wired with explosives and remote control detonators. We hadn't counted on this."

"Then all of them are Americans?"

"They could have switched clothes with some of them. We don't know yet."

The radio sounded crisply, "We're moving."

Through the failing daylight, a small convoy of vehicles could be seen moving slowly towards the small group of refugees as they walked further from the plane towards the terminal. A moment later, the radios again broke the tense silence. "All twelve are hostages. We have definite visual IDs—all are hostages!"

In the distance, the convoy split and formed a rolling half moon, partially surrounding and protecting the small group, as it grew steadily closer. "We have vocal contact. They say they are not carrying any devices."

"What about the terrorists?" muttered Mader, raising his radio to his lips. "This is Mader," he said impatiently. "I want those people isolated from everybody! Move in and take them into custody. I want no contact with anyone until they are debriefed."

"Sir, we have three injuries. One looks serious."

"Who are they?"

"The pilot is the worst, the other is Conally, and the third is our eleventh man. Their wounds appear minor. Over."

"Put an agent with the pilot and get him to San Francisco General. Put the other two in the unmarked van, and meet me in front of the terminal."

"Understood."

"Mader, clear."

As Agent Mader turned to leave, McWilliams stepped in front of him, blocking his path. "That eleventh man is my boss. Mind if I come along?"

Hesitating for a moment, Mader nodded, "Let's go. We'll have to work fast if we're going to keep this quiet."

Passing through the lobby, Mac reached down and hooked his saddle behind the pommel, then expertly swung it over his shoulder. With his left hand, he grabbed one suitcase, as Bishop took the second. Using uniformed policemen as a shield, they cut through the crowd and out to the sidewalk. Two minutes later, a dark van slid to a stop in front of them, and the passenger door swung open.

"Get in the front seat, McWilliams," said Mader, deftly taking the saddle and suitcase from McWilliams and heading for the rear of the disguised ambulance. Opening the rear doors, he paused to glance at the wounded men, his eyes holding curiously on Burkhart, as he tossed in the luggage. Then, as the third agent crawled in next to the saddle, he said in a low tone, "Take them to the University Hospital on Parnassus."

As the doors slammed shut, the tires burned the pavement, lunging the van away from the curb and into the empty street. In seconds, it was out of sight.

Watching the ambulance disappear, Agent Mader turned to his junior officer. "I don't know what the hell happened out there, but you can bet your life that number eleven is responsible. I hope he makes it," he said, then reached for his radio. "This is Mader. Move in on the plane."

"Sir, say again," responded a surprised officer.

"On my authority, take the plane!"

CHAPTER SIX

With no one following, the van merged smoothly onto the freeway and joined the flow of traffic in the fast lane. Making no attempt to exceed the speed limit, it blended instantly into the long procession of commuters. McWilliams turned in his seat to see Burkhart's bleeding forearm being wrapped by an attendant.

"Wasn't sure I was going to see you again, Boss," he said with a cordial smile. Thought I might already be out of a job."

Burkhart glanced up, his face relaxed, but pale. "You just about were," he replied evenly, then paused. "Maybe that might not be a bad idea, anyway."

Mac waved his hand, "Save your breath, Boss. I can put two and two together. I know what happened out there, more or less, and I know what it means if it gets out. I signed on for the job, and I'm stayin' for whatever comes."

"Thanks, Mac. I think I'm going to need some help."

"Hold that compress down firmly," suggested the attendant to Burkhart, "I believe the bullet missed the bone." Shifting his attention to Conally, he continued, "I need to look at this head wound."

Motioning towards the big man next to him, Burkhart smiled. "You've already met Mr. Conally, Mac. John, this is Travis McWilliams. He's my foreman."

Conally raised a finger in recognition as the attendant held his head steady and peered into both eyes with an ophthalmoscope.

"John's the one that saved your job for you out there, Mac."

"That right, John?" asked McWilliams.

"Not hardly," muttered Conally, somewhat shaken. "It happened so fast, I really don't remember much."

For a moment, Burkhart stared ahead blankly as his eyes narrowed and his face darkened. "I'm sorry for the pilot," he said remorsefully. "I don't think he's going to live. And it may have been me that shot him."

As a white bandage was being wrapped around his head, Conally took a long worried look at Burkhart, then glanced at McWilliams, who obviously shared the same concern.

"The FBI fella's goin' to try and keep exactly what happened from gettin' out," began Mac gently. "I don't know if he can do it, though. Right now, they don't have much on you as far as background, but the longer we stick around, the more that's goin' to change."

Burkhart nodded, as if half-listening.

"Jason," said McWilliams, more forcefully, "how's the arm?"

Coming out of his daze, Burkhart answered slowly. "It's a little numb, but it's not broken. The lead passed through into—I'll be fine."

"Good! We need to be getting on—as soon as we can," said McWilliams, then added emphatically, "and the sooner, the better! Do you still have my pieces?"

The last question brought Burkhart back to full awareness, as well as alerting Conally. "Yes. I still have them," said Burkhart.

"What you said on the plane—about wanting your privacy—made sense, Jason," announced the big man, while nonchalantly pointing with his eyes at the Federal agent next to him. "And it sounds like Travis has the same sort of idea. You can count on my help, anytime."

Turning toward McWilliams, out of view of the FBI agent, Burkhart rubbed his arm, but pointed with his fingers at the driver. "John knows how important it is for us to get back home, too, and pronto. He's agreed to take the heel—and you take the head—just like team roping."

"Well now, John," acknowledged McWilliams. "You'll do, after all! You handle your end, and I'll handle mine."

In the quiet of the next few minutes, only the hum of the engine and the clatter of the attendant cleaning up were heard, but the sudden ticking of a turn signal warned of a lane change, and soon the van began to decelerate. Coming to a stop at the bottom of an off ramp, McWilliams twisted in his seat, and said calmly, "Now, boys!"

Instantly, two huge arms encircled the FBI agent, pinning his arms at his sides as Burkhart tossed one of the pistols to McWilliams. Grabbing the agent's snub-nose from its shoulder holster, Burkhart covered the medical attendant as McWilliams shoved the old Colt against the ribs of the driver and smiled politely. "You're gettin' out here."

"What do you think you're doing?" shouted the agent, in wide-eyed amazement.

"Protecting our own, sir," replied McWilliams. "Just doin' what we have to."

Pointing with the revolver, Burkhart indicated the rear doors. "Everybody—out the back."

Still clutching the agent, Conally asked, "What do you want me to do?"

Holding the pistol out to him, Burkhart answered, "Keep them away from a phone or a radio as long as you can."

"I understand," replied Conally, releasing one hand to open the rear door. After accepting the snub-nosed pistol from Burkhart, he shoved the attendant and the driver out first, and then lifted the agent as if he were a doll, and stepped outside. "Good luck," he said sincerely. "And thanks. If it weren't for you, it would have been me lying out there on that runway."

"You had the luck," muttered Burkhart. "Explain to the pilot. Tell him—it was the only thing I could do."

At a loss for words, he reached for the doors, paused, and then pulled them shut. "God, help that pilot," he pleaded softly as he went to the front of the van and took the passenger seat.

"Which way, Boss? East?" asked McWilliams, now behind the wheel.

"Straight ahead, and back on the freeway. We've got to get rid of this van, first. We'll rent a car up ahead, then go east," explained Burkhart. "It'll be dark in a few minutes. That will help. We need four hours to make it to Nevada."

"I think we got a good shot at makin' it. I halfway believe that Agent Mader figured we'd make a break for it."

"Who?"

"The FBI fella back there that seemed to be runnin' the whole operation," replied McWilliams as the van merged into the right lane of the freeway. "He was trying to keep your name a secret, not give it to the papers and television."

"Do you think he can?"

After a long minute, Mac answered confidently, "He's got a good chance at it." Reaching for the radio, he added, "Let's see how he's doin' so far."

For the next several miles, they listened to station after station as each reported the story as it had unfolded up to the point of the hostage's mysterious release. As yet, none had mentioned any wounded, nor the names of anyone that had been on board. What had happened to the terrorists was still a matter of speculation that presently consumed most of the airtime.

Turning the volume down low, Burkhart motioned with his right hand, now crusted with dried blood. "Take the next exit. There's a rental place across from the off ramp," he said, then anxiously added, "I wish I knew how the pilot was doing."

"We'll hear soon enough. How are you doin'?"

"I can't describe how I feel, Mac. I don't even recognize what's going on inside me—except to say it makes me feel sick to my stomach."

Coming off the freeway to a stop sign, McWilliams' brow wrinkled, his eyes staring at something distant. "I was in some nasty scrapes in the Viet Nam war. We did some things—saw some things—I believe I know how you feel. It had to be done, though. I had to believe that then, and you have to believe the same thing now. You did what you had to. Don't second-guess yourself, Jason. Just go on with your life, and leave it alone."

Shaking his head slowly, Burkhart replied, "I'm afraid that's going to take a while. I have an idea the end of all this is a long way off."

Looking to his left, McWilliams asked, "That the rental place over there?"

"Yes. We'd better rent the car in your name. It may buy us some time."

"Likely it will, Boss. But the FBI has a mighty long arm. They'll eventually find us."

"I know. It's not them I'm worried about. Right now, I just want time and distance—to get back to my ranch. I just want to get back to Nevada, to the desert. At least there, I can think while they're looking for me. If the media finds out anything, I won't have a minute to myself, or the slightest chance of escaping retaliation. I'll have no life at all—just when it seemed like it was starting to come back."

"Could be they may not come at you at all."

Burkhart sighed. "I used to be a paramedic in San Francisco. Between calls, I did a lot of reading and kept up with all the news and talk shows, especially since 9-11. At the station, all of us studied what the terrorists were doing—how they operated. It was part of our job. They will retaliate, if they can. That's what they do. It's part of their culture."

McWilliams frowned. "All the more important we get back home as quiet as we can. And so far, so good."

Pulling into the rental agency, McWilliams parked in an obscure corner and went in. A few minutes later, he drove up behind the van in a non-descript sedan and turned off his headlights.

As Mac unloaded his gear from the rear, Burkhart took a careful look around the parking area and the main office. Easing open the door, he took a deep breath, then stepped into the dim light and damp evening air.

The airport cafeteria was brightly lit, but the tables were bare, and except for a handful of young athletes and a few men in dark business suits, the room was empty. From the rear, a door was heard to open, then the hollow sound of shoe heels echoed off the walls, breaking a long silence.

Making his way down an aisle was Agent Mader; following closely behind was Dr. Webb. The former hostages, now sitting side by side in a row of chairs, turned to see who had entered, then watched suspiciously as the two men advanced.

Coming around to stand in front of them, Mader introduced himself. “My name is Mader. I’m the Special-Agent-in-Charge, FBI. I’m here to debrief you. This is Dr. Webb.” Mader’s lips tightened, then he continued mechanically. “He’s here—to aid you in adjusting to any psychological trauma you may have endured.

“First of all though, we need to know just what happened out there, and why. Who can tell me how the shooting started?”

A moment passed, and no one responded. Some of the younger men nervously averted their eyes, while others stared ahead blankly. A few, feigning boredom, slumped lazily in their seats.

“Okay,” said Mader patiently. “Let’s start at the beginning. Tell me about the terrorists. What were they like once you were aboard? How were you treated?”

Again, there was no response, and Mader turned questioningly to Webb. Looking just as perplexed, Webb merely shrugged his shoulders. After pacing the floor a few times, Mader tried once more.

"Gentleman, let me tell you, here and now, that this investigation is for the FBI anti-terrorist task force. We are not giving any of this information to the press. If you wish to discuss these matters with them afterwards, that's your privilege, but what you say here and now is strictly for national security.

"And let me tell you how much we do know already—there were eleven of you abducted. Nine of you are here, one of your number was wounded, and still another did not, in fact, belong with you at all. We know his name and that he had two pistols with him when he was taken."

Mader took a moment to study the nine faces carefully, then added, "And we want to do what we can to protect that eleventh man, but we need information in order to do that."

Suddenly, and without exception, the faces before him registered surprise, and Mader knew he had guessed correctly. "Now, what can you tell me?"

Looking from one to another, the athletes exchanged glances of uncertainty and whispered back and forth, until all seemed agreed. "It all happened so fast," offered a short but stocky player, "It was over in just a few seconds."

"And your name, please?"

"Rossman."

"Thank you, Mr. Rossman. Tell me what you saw."

"I was sitting kind of in the back, on the left side of the plane, one seat in front of John Conally. This other guy was across from me, one seat back. He seemed to be working on something each time the guard went to the front of the plane, but at the time, I didn't think much of it. I was hardly able to think of anything. Anyway, when they took John up to the front door, this guy stood up and fired into the guard standing in front of him. And—uh—uh—"

"Yes, Mr. Rossman?" encouraged Mader.

"He spun that guard around and held him in front of his body with his left arm around his neck. Then he shot at the guard that was standing behind John, but I think he missed the first time. Before that other guard could aim his machine gun at him, John turned around and slapped the gun up in the air, and the shots went into the ceiling. Then the guy with the pistols shot two or three times, real fast, and the guard went down. I think that's when he went out the door and fell."

"And the other three terrorists?" prompted Mader eagerly.

"Yeah—about that time, the place was full of smoke from those old guns, the door to where the pilot was flew open, and two more terrorists ran out. They must not have been able to see, for the smoke, because they didn't start shooting right off, but the other guy sure did. I think he only shot twice, and they both dropped. But by then, I was on the floor and didn't see what else happened."

"Well, I sure as hell did!" said a tall, well-built young man.

"Name?"

"Tucker."

"Go on, Mr. Tucker."

"The first two dropped, alright. I was sitting in the front row, and one of them fell on top of me. The next thing that happened was the pilot came through the door, like he was pushed through. Right behind him came the last terrorist, but he was ready. By then, the smoke was all the way up to where we were. I guess he didn't see our guy very well, because he didn't get off the first shot. The terrorist got hit but didn't go down, and then he started shooting everything in sight. I know he hit the pilot, but he only wounded the guy shooting back at him, because our guy fired five or six more times. I forget. Then it went quiet, and we couldn't see for all the smoke. Those damned pistols really belched it out!"

"And then what?"

"We tried to help the pilot the best we could, or I should say, the guy with the pistols did—you should have seen him work. He knew what he was doing."

"How long did that take?"

Tucker shrugged. "A couple of minutes, I guess. I don't know. While he was working on the pilot, the guy was talking to us."

"About what?"

Tucker hesitated, then said cautiously, "He asked us not to talk to anyone about what had happened. He said he just wanted to be left alone, and didn't want any part of what just happened. He said if it got out who had done the shooting, he could be hunted down and killed by other terrorists. And we all agreed to do it, too."

"Why did you agree to that request, Mr. Tucker?" asked Webb.

"Why?" blurted Rossman. "For one thing, we believe what he said about his being marked for death. It's no secret how these assholes think."

"And for another thing," replied a third voice, "he saved Conally's life. He said he just wanted to be left alone, and we think he should get what he wants!"

"How do you know he saved Conally's life, Mr.—?" questioned Mader.

"Hardy. Greg Hardy. I know because they had put a gun to the back of his head and told him to kneel down."

Webb's eyes narrowed analytically. "Did you hear them say they were actually going to shoot at that moment?"

"No. They didn't speak English, except when they ordered us around."

Looking vaguely pleased with the answer, Webb continued, "Then you are only assuming what they intended to do."

After a moment of silence, Rossman spoke up defiantly. "Nobody had to tell us what they were going to do. You could see it in their faces. You could feel it."

"I see," replied Webb patronizingly. "You must all understand it is perfectly normal to feel threatened when your freedom is taken from you in a violent manner. And it is predictable that each of you, at this point in time, sees Mr. Burthark as a savior. However, in a few days—or even a few hours—you may begin to see the circumstances of your release in a different light. You may even experience guilt feelings for having held this man in such high regard as you begin to understand what he has done. It is important that you do not blame yourselves, in any way, for condoning the premature and irresponsible actions that led to the death of four human beings and the serious injury, or even death, of the pilot."

Irritably, Agent Mader glared at Webb, then turned his attention back to the athletes. "Thank you, Dr. Webb," he said, suppressing his animosity. "Did the terrorists, at any time, identify themselves?"

"Just before they took Conally to the front," said Rossman, "I heard them say something about the Alliance for Greater Syria."

"That's a new one," snarled Mader. "That means they could have been from Syria, Lebanon or Jordan—or even all three places. In the Middle East, you never know who is going to crawl into bed with whom."

Dr. Webb took a step forward. "Let me encourage you to contact me should you begin experiencing any symptoms of depression—excessive nervousness, sleeplessness, or guilt. Post-traumatic stress disorder may take many forms, but with proper counseling, full recovery is the norm."

As Webb spoke, a messenger entered the cafeteria and went directly to Mader, handing him a written note. After reading it, Mader stuck it in his pocket. "You are free to go now," he said. "Transportation has been arranged to take you to your homes or back to the college. Let me warn you that you are going to be hounded by reporters trying to get a story. But remember what you went through today and the man whose life you hold in your hands. Until we can fully protect him, be absolutely certain you keep his name to yourselves. Goodnight, gentlemen."

As the room cleared, Mader checked his watch. He then motioned for Bishop to come over. "Check on the condition of the pilot and report back to me here."

"Yes, sir. How about the other two? Burkhart and Conally?"

"Never mind them. I just got word—they're both more than healthy."

After Agent Bishop left the room, only Mader and Webb remained. As the doctor started for the exit, Mader stopped him. "Dr. Webb, correct me if I'm wrong, but it seems you are quiet prejudiced against our eleventh man. Why is that?"

"Prejudiced? I hardly think so," answered Webb evasively.

"You sound like you've decided what he did out there was wrong and were trying to convince the hostages of the same thing."

"I believe it was reckless and irresponsible. It serves as an excellent illustration of how frontier mentality and gun ownership are inevitably linked and have no place in our modern society."

"I take it you are an advocate of gun control?"

"I believe only the military and law enforcement personnel should be allowed to carry firearms. That is the 'control' I advocate. If Burthark had not possessed those pistols, the pilot would not be in critical condition, and the needless deaths of four other men would have been prevented. It rather proves my point, does it not?"

Unwrapping a piece of gum, Mader popped it into his mouth, exhaling heavily as he chewed. "Thanks for coming down tonight, Dr. Webb. I know your time is valuable. From here on out, I'm going to assign a departmental psychologist to these boys, and you can return to your busy schedule."

Fish-like, Webb's mouth dropped open, for the moment rendering him speechless. Then a deep shade of red burned across his fat jowls. "You haven't the authority to take me off this case," he stammered, with bulging eyes. "I'm on the Counter-Terrorist Advisory Committee!"

Agent Mader savored his gum briefly, then countered, "You'd best serve the public by returning to your private practice, doctor. I can—and I will—make your reassignment stick."

"We'll see about that," snapped Webb. "You've overstepped your authority for the second time today!"

"Yeah," said Mader indifferently. "When was the first time?"

Webb smiled sadistically, but said nothing. Smugly, he adjusted his suit coat and buttoned it closed over his paunchy belly, then turned confidently and walked for the door. Passing Bishop on his way out, he mumbled snidely to himself, "The public has a right to know!"

Mader held up his hand to Bishop until the door had closed completely, then asked, "What did you find out?"

"It looks bad for the pilot. He isn't going to make it."

Mader swore under his breath. "What do you know about this Dr. Webb?"

"Not much. Some sort of a big wheel shrink in the city. Gives lectures at the colleges, sometimes gets himself on television—that sort of thing. The word from headquarters is that he's got friends in high places. It seems, too, that his brother-in-law is on the city council."

"It figures!" sighed Mader. "Let's get some fresh air."

Behind the airport's cafeteria, parked next to a large trash bin, were two dark sedans, now covered with moisture that resembled tiny beads of cold sweat. A light fog drifted in the darkness, adding a penetrating chill to the night air.

"Burkhart and McWilliams made a break for it," said Mader, as he flipped up the collar of his coat. "Took the unmarked ambulance and left the rest of them on a street corner—with Conally's help."

“Did they hurt anyone?” asked Bishop calmly.

“No. Apparently, they were very polite about the whole thing. Why is it you don’t seem surprised, Agent Bishop?”

“Well sir, like you said—it figures. That old fella was crusty, and even though he couldn’t have much of an education, he seemed a lot smarter than that psychologist back there. He never was intimidated, and stood toe to toe with him a couple of times. As for Burkhart, it seems that a lot of things, and maybe some people, might turn against him if he was to stick around. If I were him, and thought I had half a chance, I’d have done the same thing. What do you make of his chances? How much did they get on him with the computer?”

“That’s a point in his favor,” answered Mader. “The computer came up empty, and I confiscated the video of the incident. I would say he has a fair chance. I want you to check a hundred mile radius for a rental vehicle to a Burkhart or McWilliams. If they’re smart, they won’t stay in the van long.” Opening his car door, Mader paused and smiled. “And Bishop—take your time; report only to me. We’ve been dreading this day for years, wondering what we’d do if this kind of terrorism started here at home. I personally think Burkhart did the whole country a favor, and may have single-handedly stopped a Jihad before it could get off the ground. The least we can do is give him some breathing room.”

“Understood, sir,” grinned Bishop. “Understood!”

CHAPTER SEVEN

Just past the Oakland Bay Bridge, Burkhart discovered the rental car's radio was inoperable; for the last hour, they had been completely cut off from any sort of news. With no idea what was happening with the attempted kidnapping, Burkhart had been consumed with his own thoughts. McWilliams, out of courtesy and concern, had remained quiet. But as they approached the next town, Burkhart sat up and rubbed his palms against his weary, bloodshot eyes. "Cowtown," he mumbled.

"What's that?"

"Cowtown. Vacaville means 'Cowtown' in Spanish. It also means we're getting closer to home."

"How much further?"

"Oh, it's three hours just to get to the Nevada border," answered Burkhart with a forced smile. "But the thought of cows makes me feel better. Let's take this next exit and get off here in town. I'm getting hungry, and I could use some aspirin."

"Being hungry—that's a good sign, Boss!" offered McWilliams enthusiastically. "You're goin' to do just fine. And now that you mention it, I'm pretty hungry, too. We'll both feel a lot better with something to eat and a couple of cups of strong coffee."

After taking the off ramp, they drove a short distance to a small diner, and quietly took a seat at the end of the counter. Before they could open the menus, a young waitress hurried over with a pot of coffee. "Hi stranger," she said, in a loud but friendly voice. "Haven't seen you in a quite a while! What have you been up to lately?"

"Yes, it's been a long time," answered Burkhart, somewhat surprised to see a familiar face. "I don't come this way as often as I used to. I thought you only worked the day shift."

"Sure. I still do, but one of the girls ran off and got married, so I'm filling in until they get somebody else. What do you boys want tonight?"

After taking their orders to go, the waitress left, and McWilliams leaned into Burkhart's ear. "Does she know you?" he asked, puzzled.

"Not by name. I used to stop here and eat quite a bit when I was looking over the ranches in Nevada. I had no idea she'd be here tonight. I'll have to be more careful in the future."

"You got that right, Boss," agreed McWilliams, as he looked over the humble décor of the restaurant. "How's the food here?"

"There are fancier places around, but what this place doesn't have in atmosphere, it makes up for in cooking. And they're genuinely friendly here."

A few minutes later, the waitress returned with two brown sacks and two large, white Styrofoam cups with lids. "Two cheeseburger specials, and two coffees to go," she announced as she set the load down. "Have the two of you been following that thing that happened over at the San Francisco airport?"

"We've heard some about it," answered Mac dryly. "But our car radio is busted."

"Bill, our cook, has the TV on back there. Says somebody's called a news conference to tell what all went on. It should be on in a second."

"The last we heard," said Burkhart mildly, "was that the hostages had been released. And I believe a pilot was injured."

The waitress nodded as she rang up the bill. "Yeah, it was sure strange how they all got away like that. I don't recall anything like that ever happening before—or anything about the pilot, either."

Suddenly a baritone Texas drawl boomed from the kitchen. “You gotta be kiddin’ me!”

For a moment, the diner went quiet as every one froze in place, but the young waitress merely shook her head tolerantly and waved a reassuring hand. “You folks go on and eat. That was just the cook blowing off steam. Happens all the time.”

After a round of chuckles rippled through the diner, the waitress’ flat smile faded. “What on earth is he bellowing about now?” she whispered, then spun on her heels and headed for the kitchen.

Mac picked up his sack and coffee, but Burkhart shook his head. “Hang on for a second. I want to see what happened.”

A long two minutes later, the waitress rounded the corner from the kitchen, looking perplexed. “You’re never going to guess what’s going on with that airplane deal,” she said, as if mystified. “Turns out some guy took pistols on when he was kidnapped and ended up shooting all five terrorists. But the pilot got shot, too, and isn’t expected to live. So now they’re going to try and have the guy arrested for something called ‘public endangerment’—and, get this—having a concealed weapon without a permit!”

Mac stood, dumbfounded, but Burkhart swallowed hard, and asked, “Did they say who it was that did the shooting, or where he was?”

“Yeah, they did. The FBI is holding him, and they said his name, but I can’t remember, Jason something or other. But don’t that beat all? That damned San Francisco is a freak show by the Bay.”

Recovering from the initial shock, McWilliams asked heatedly, “Who gave that press conference, anyway?”

“Oh, some city counsel big-wig and the wife of the pilot. And there was another guy standing next to them, short, fat—with a goatee.”

“Webb!” sneered McWilliams, without thinking.

“That was it,” agreed the waitress. “Dr. Webb—how’d you know?”

Mac's eyes widened. "I think—I heard somewhere that he was the psychologist for some terrorist task force for the airport."

"Well, I guess that clears that up," Burkhart said, as he reached for his order. "I was wondering how that ended. Now we know."

Looking at Burkhart curiously, the waitress paused. "You're from the Bay Area. What do you think about arresting that man? He shot all those terrorists, but the pilot may die. I can see Bobby's point—that's the cook—about self-defense and all, but so many times, terrorists just keep hostages for a while to make their point and then let them all go, and nobody gets hurt. Maybe that man with the pistols should have waited to see what they wanted. If it was my husband in the hospital, I might be wondering if it was all really necessary, too."

Before Burkhart could reply, a bell sounded from the kitchen. "Got to go," chirped the waitress, waving a hand. "You two come back and see us real soon."

"You've gotta expect that kind of thinkin' at first," said McWilliams reassuringly. "There's no way they can understand how it was out there. But in the long run, most people will realize they can't judge you for what you did."

"I don't know about that," replied Burkhart uneasily, as the two headed for the door. "There's a growing segment of our society that believes violence, even in the form of self-defense, shouldn't be tolerated, but should be a matter for the police. They live in so much fear of being shot they're trying to make all gun ownership illegal. That group's well organized in San Francisco and supported by the media and the city council. Those people can get a whole army of lawyers after me. They'll crucify me and make it sound like I got off easy! They'll want to make an example out of me. You know: cowboy equals vigilante."

"Maybe in San Francisco, or even California, in general," replied McWilliams. "But don't go sellin' the American people short. You've been livin' in 'the land of fruits and nuts' too long. There's a whole lot of folks, a majority, who are gettin' fed up with the media and can still think for themselves. They'll side with you because they're Americans. Real Americans believe in freedom, self-defense, and the right to fight for it. You wait and see, Jason. When it's all said and done, you'll come out on top."

Five miles down the freeway, Burkhart anxiously glanced over his shoulder at a car that was following too close. "It was seven-fifteen when we left the restaurant," he said, thinking aloud. "They'll be tracing me back to New Mexico, by now. Maybe even to the tour. And then—"

"We better be getting off this main road," interrupted McWilliams. "You know any other way into Nevada?"

"When we get to Sacramento, we'll take Highway 16 into the hills. From there, 88 will take us over Carson Pass and down into Nevada. Before they can trace me to Nevada, I think we'll be there. But it's best to be on the safe side."

"Sounds good to me. How far to Sacramento?"

"About thirty miles to where we pick up 16. Until then, we have to hope they haven't found the van and already have a description of this car."

McWilliams glanced in the rear view mirror, then at the speedometer to check his speed for the slow lane. "Now that you bring it up, I just thought of something."

"What?"

"If that waitress got her story right, she said they were reportin' you to still be in the hands of the Feds. And you ain't been there for over an hour."

"Do you think Conally has held them off that long?" asked Burkhart.

"I doubt it, Boss. Somethin' else is goin' on—something mighty peculiar."

For several miles, they drove in silence, paying little attention to the stream of cars passing on their left or the countless pairs of red taillights in front of them, but as the specks of red began to flash brightly, McWilliams eased his foot off the gas pedal.

"The traffic gets heavy through here," said Burkhart. "The turnoff is about three miles up."

"Have you thought about what the Feds will find if they trace you back to Nevada?"

"Just what I've been thinking about, myself," answered Burkhart, his brow wrinkled in concentration. "I took the flight out of Reno and paid cash for it. Virtually no one knows that I moved from San Francisco, or if they do, they don't know where I went. I didn't use a bank when I bought the ranch, and it hasn't been in my name but a few months. Nevada is an unpopulated, wide-open country. It might take months before they find the ranch, and by then, things may have changed for the better."

"Sounds encouraging to me, Boss. Is that our exit coming up there?"

"Yes. One mile ahead, the traffic gets heavy. Just stay in the right lane, and we'll be okay."

As the traffic slowed, McWilliams braked gently, then glanced in the rearview mirror. The car behind him, silhouetted by a string of bright headlights, had a familiar outline, and as he slowed again, his heart began to race. "We've got trouble," he choked. "Take a look behind us."

Burkhart squinted over his shoulder just as the red and blue lights of the patrol car flashed on. A nauseating jolt hit the pit of his stomach, and he slowly turned back around, feeling very tired.

"We could try to lose 'em," offered McWilliams.

"No—there's no need to endanger your life, or anyone else's over this," replied Burkhart wearily. "Just pull over. It was all just wishful thinking. But I had no idea they would find us so fast."

After pulling to the side of the freeway, McWilliams rolled down his window as the highway patrolman approached. On a metallic green highway sign, a few feet in front of them, 'Highway 16, ¼ mile' was reflected in large white letters.

"May I see your driver's license, please?" requested the officer. As McWilliams handed it over, the officer asked, "Do you know why you were stopped?"

"Well, I don't believe there was anything wrong with what we did," answered McWilliams defensively.

For a moment, the officer did not reply. Then, after studying Travis McWilliams for a long count of ten, he leaned over to look at Burkhart. After another extended pause, he said blandly, "Your left brake light isn't working. May I see the registration?"

"Taillight?" repeated McWilliams in disbelief. "You stopped us for a taillight?"

"Officer, we rented this car," offered Burkhart, trying to sound relaxed. "Would a receipt from the rental company do?"

"I'll take a look at it," replied the patrolman, his eyes fixed on Burkhart. "Where are you headed?"

"East. Maybe as far as Tahoe," answered Burkhart.

Taking the piece of paper, the officer checked it with his flashlight, then handed it back. "Remember that if your brake light is out, so is your turn signal. Be careful Mr. McWilliams—and welcome to California." After replacing his flashlight, the patrolman stooped over once more to peer inside. "Were you two going to take that Highway 16 exit?"

McWilliams glanced at Burkhart who, for a moment, studied the officer. "Is it a good road?"

"50 and 80 are going to be busy tonight, probably for the next few days. People that value their time would be better off on the back roads. And it will be a safer way to go."

"That's good advice," said Burkhart graciously. "And—thank you very much."

The patrol car remained behind them until the state highway exit, then vanished from view as they left the freeway and rolled onto State Highway16.

"Nice fella," laughed McWilliams with relief. "I thought we was sunk, for sure. We didn't even get so much as a ticket. Things are lookin' up!"

"They sure are, Mac. Especially since Interstate 80 and 50 don't get tied up this time of year."

"But he said they was—goin' to be busy," replied McWilliams, then glanced at Burkhart. "You mean, you think he knew? He knew who you were?"

"I'm sure of it. And he knew about you too, but he let us go. Not only did he let us go, but he told us where to go to avoid being caught."

"Well now!" howled Mac, as he slapped the steering wheel with his hand. "We've got some friends out there already. Hot damn. I knew it!"

Two hours past Sacramento, the rented sedan crested the summit of Kit Carson Pass and began descending rapidly through Hope Valley. By midnight, it was leveling off on the desert flats of Nevada.

Shoving both palms against the steering wheel, McWilliams arched his stiff back into the seat and blinked heavily. After a tranquilizing yawn, he shook his head, then checked his watch. "Well, we made it over the state line, and as of a few minutes ago, yesterday is now behind us."

Burkhart grunted. "It's hard to believe yesterday started only twenty-four hours ago. Seems more like a week has gone by."

"It has been a long one alright, but it's over and done with. And every passin' day will push it all further into the past. Like everything else, it'll just take time to work itself out."

Glancing at McWilliams, Burkhart noticed the drooping eyelids and haggard face. "We've got a long way to go, Mac. Why don't you let me drive awhile? I can't sleep, anyway."

Nodding wearily, McWilliams replied, "I could use the sleep, but what about your arm?"

"It's stiff, but I'll be fine. I can always hold the wheel with my knee if I need to use my right arm for anything."

McWilliams yawned again. "We could stop at a motel."

Burkhart shook his head. "There won't be any for a couple of hours, and besides, we can't afford the risk. We need to at least get to Fallon before we slow down. I left my pickup there and took a bus to the airport. Once we get rid of this car, I'll feel a whole lot better."

"You're the boss," agreed Mac, as he came to a smooth stop in the middle of the highway.

Stepping into the cool night, Burkhart paused to enjoy the familiar smell of sage and stared up at a star crowded blue-black sky. An owl's wings flickered in the reflected light of the car as something small scurried safely into the brush beyond the shoulder of the road.

"Nothin' like a desert night," said McWilliams, sliding over to the passenger's side. "Somethin' about 'em gets in your blood."

Feeling a gentle breeze brush his cheek, Burkhart smiled to himself. "It's nice to be away from all the lights. It helps keep things in perspective."

Circling around the rear of the car, he opened the door. Taking one last look at the stars, he filled his lungs with crisp clean air, then, guarding his injured arm, carefully took his seat.

"How long'd you say it was to Fallon?" asked McWilliams, keeping a concerned eye on Burkhart as he shifted into gear and accelerated.

"Close to three hours. You go ahead and get as much sleep as you can. I'll wake you if I need you."

Satisfied that Burkhart could drive, McWilliams slumped into the seat and sluggishly leaned his head back. After adjusting his hat down over his eyes, he folded his arms and was instantly asleep.

With the pain in his arm beginning to subside, and his immediate problems behind him, Jason Burkhart turned his attention to what lay ahead. As the headlights burned a tunnel through the midnight blackness, he groped with the complexity of his bizarre situation.

Admittedly, his chances were dim, if existent at all, but still he would have to have a plan and take every precaution to protect his identity. If he were to be exposed as the eleventh man—he must ultimately be prepared for the worst.

Overshadowing the uncertainties of legal prosecution was the ominous threat of reprisal, a threat that would become a certainty if he were located. Yet could he possibly hope to get away, to actually disappear in the vastness of the Nevada deserts? Would charges against him in the city of San Francisco stand against him in Nevada, or would the FBI take over the investigation and make it a federal matter?

Step by step, mile by mile, Burkhart gradually pieced together a meticulous prediction of what would occur should his whereabouts become known. Ignoring any legal action against him for the time being, he considered every conceivable defensive strategy. But as the hours passed, his options grew fewer and fewer, until finally, only one remained.

He would retreat no further than Austin. He had no desire to go into hiding, nor could he find it within himself to do so. What he had done on the plane was simply what had to be done. Anything else, for him, was unthinkable. And what he must do now was just as clear.

There would be no cowering in fear, no pitiful hoping to merely survive. As it was for him on the plane, so it was now. There was only one pathway open to him, and he gravely accepted what his fate would be, should his location be discovered. He would take no unnecessary chances, but if they wanted him, they would have to face him. His life would not be stolen by a cowardly act of terrorism. There would be a price to pay, and he intended to collect on his own terms. If he was to be killed, it would be in the desert—the desert he had sought to bring him peace, the sanctuary that had nurtured him through tragedy, and now, regrettably, the land that had introduced him to Kimberly Whitney.

When he was first taken captive, there was no time to think of her. When Conally was knocked to the floor, there was no time to do anything but help. But for a moment, as he was loading the pistols behind the seat of the plane, he saw her face and heard her voice. From that moment until now, he had forced her from his mind.

Flying from Nevada to New Mexico, he had thought of her constantly and what their brief encounters meant. He knew, from the beginning of the flight, that he was looking forward to seeing Kimberly again, but before landing in Gallup, admitted his desire to be with her was more than a casual interest. In fact, he realized it was much more. Now, however, driving through the black of night, Jason Burkhart had to put an end to the dream. To protect Kimberly Whitney, those feelings were to be buried.

Ten minutes from Fallon, McWilliams stirred. Smacking his lips, he raised his hat and half-opened one eye. "We 'bout there?"

"Another twelve miles. Feel better?"

Extending his wiry arms behind his head, McWilliams groaned and stretched. "Lots better," he answered. "A few hours can go a long ways when there's a need."

"It's good you got some sleep. The cab of the pickup is too small to stretch out in."

Sitting upright, and rubbing the grit from his eyes, McWilliams cleared his throat with a raspy cough. "What are we going to do with this car, anyways?"

"I'm going to get rid of it for a while. If they find the car here, they'll know we're in Nevada for sure, and that we can't afford."

"What do you mean, 'get rid of it for a while'?"

Burkhart grinned slyly. "I had a mechanic do some work on my truck in Fallon last month. What should have taken him an hour, ended up being an all day job.

"We'll leave the car at his garage, park it out back. I'll leave a note on it to rebuild the engine; since it has ninety thousand miles on it, he won't question it. That'll bury the car for at least a month, if not longer."

"Now that's pretty slick," chuckled McWilliams. "Any chance of gettin' coffee in this town?"

"I don't know it that well. I hope so, but in these small towns, you never can tell. If we don't find any, I'm going to let you drive to Austin. I think I could sleep now, even in the truck. Besides, it's a stick shift, and I doubt I could handle it with this arm. It would start to bleed again. And the transmission has—has what you might call a temperamental personality, too. I'll have to guide you through it a couple of times, but you'll get the hang of it."

"Sounds interestin'. What kind of truck is it?"

"It's a 1954 Willys Overland. It's a rugged old truck that came with the ranch, but I've worked on it quite a bit since then. Now, at the very least, it's dependable."

On the outskirts of Fallon, Burkhart slowed to thirty-five as both men searched for an all-night coffee shop, but the town was closed up tight. Halfway through the business district, they turned left into a dimly lit parking lot with a dark-colored pickup parked next to a half dozen dust-covered vehicles.

"That your truck?" asked McWilliams.

"That's it," affirmed Burkhart as he came to a stop and slid his hand into his pocket for the key. Handing it to McWilliams, he added, "There are four gear shifts on the floor. The one nearest the driver is a standard three speed, with reverse at the top. We'll go over the others after we get to the garage."

McWilliams nodded and pushed open his door. As he put his foot out, Burkhart stopped him. "One more thing.

You have to choke it all the way out to start it, and the choke is to the right on the dash board."

A moment later, with McWilliams behind the wheel, the Willys snapped to a start, and after a short warm-up followed the sedan back out onto the main street. Several blocks later, they turned down a dingy side street, and then into an alley that led to what appeared to be a junkyard for used cars.

Burkhart quickly pulled into an empty space and turned off the sedan's engine as McWilliams drove in behind him, using only his parking lights. After loading their few belongings in the bed of the truck, Burkhart found a stained piece of cardboard. Kneeling in front of the pickup lights, he wrote out his instructions to the mechanic.

"If you can clip this under the windshield wipers, Mac, we'll be all set."

Taking the cardboard, McWilliams started for the car, then stopped and looked back. "What about the keys?"

"I put them under the mat, but you might check the glove compartment for anything that might indicate the car's a rental. He'll just think I bought myself a used car. I wrote that I was in no hurry to get it repaired—or paid for. They'll never find it."

Taking one last look around, Burkhart stepped into the small cab and eased the door shut. Then, leaning across the seat, he lifted the inside door handle and pushed it open for McWilliams.

"It tends to stick from the outside," he said, in response to Mac's curious glance. "Let's get back on Main Street before I go over the gears. The sooner we're away from that rental, the better I'll feel."

"Me too, Boss, me too," agreed McWilliams as he eased the truck into reverse and backed out into the alley.

Driving slowly east through the remainder of downtown Fallon, Burkhart pointed to the four stick shifts. "Like I said, the one furthest to the left is the standard three-speed. The next one over is overdrive. Next to it is what puts it into four-wheel drive. All those mixed together give you twenty-four different gear combinations."

"You're kiddin'!"

"No. The truck is old, but it's one of the most versatile and durable ever built. It will do more than most people would ever imagine—only it takes some practice. At first it seems complicated, but after a little while it's easy."

"When do we use the overdrive?"

"As soon as we're out of town. After you're in third gear, just shift forward. We're on Main Street now, but it's also Highway 50. It'll take you straight to Austin, and there's no chance of getting lost. It's the only road out here. In fact, it's so isolated, they've named this stretch the 'Loneliest Road in America.'"

"Sounds simple enough for now," said McWilliams. "How far to Austin?"

"Actually, we'll be going a few miles past Austin to Dry Creek Road. That's one hundred miles from here," answered Burkhart as he closed his eyes. "One hundred long and empty miles."

The eastern sky was pale yellow when McWilliams pulled off the pavement, heading north on Dry Creek Rd. To the right and left were miles of sage that, even in the dim light, already cast their peculiar blue-green colors across the landscape. In the headlights, a jackrabbit, temporarily blinded, bounded in front of them, then suddenly lunged into the darkness. With his foot on the brake, McWilliams glanced at Burkhart, waiting for him to awaken on his own.

"We on Dry Creek?" mumbled Burkhart, without moving or opening his eyes.

"Just got on it. Thought I'd better pull over until I got some more directions."

Burkhart's eyes cracked open into slits, then closed tightly and opened wider as he waited for them to focus.

"Four miles on this dirt road, then two more miles, and we're home."

"Get any sleep?"

"On and off," replied Burkhart, sitting up stiffly. "Likely more than it feels like. Once the sun hits me, I'll feel better."

Driving back onto the gravel road, McWilliams worked his way through the first set of gears, then shifted into overdrive. "What's on for today?"

"Check the place over first and see what you think. Then we'll get some breakfast and make a list of things we're going to need to stock up on in town."

"How's far's the ranch from town?"

"Just under an hour. The six miles in and out of the ranch on the dirt take some time, but the rest of the drive is easy."

Mac scratched his rough beard, thinking for a moment before he spoke. "Maybe we can get a paper while we're there and find out what went on last night, where we stand today, and such."

Rubbing both eyes with the back of his knuckles, Burkhart yawned. "Can't get a paper. Austin won't have today's newspaper until late this afternoon. I doubt we'll be there that late."

"You have a radio at the ranch?"

"Nope. Never wanted one. We'll just have to be patient and hope for the best, but get ready for the worst."

Mac shrugged uncomfortably. "Straight ahead?"

"Yeah. About four miles up, the road forks, and we go left."

Making his way around a large pothole, McWilliams shifted back into second and hunched over the steering wheel. Straining his eyes, he peered through the bug spots on the windshield, searching the horizon. "You said the ranch was in the middle of Nevada, but this looks more like the middle of nowhere to me."

Burkhart smiled. "It's not so bad. We have neighbors nine or so miles to the east of us."

"And who might that be?" snorted McWilliams good-naturedly.

His face sliding into a bland stare, Burkhart replied flatly, "It's the Whitney ranch I told you about. Run by Kimberly Whitney."

"A woman—runnin' a ranch—and out here, to boot."

"She's an exceptional woman," frowned Burkhart, as his eyes drifted towards the faint blue sky of dawn. "She raises cattle—and grows roses."

"And you said she wasn't married?" asked McWilliams, hoping to brighten the conversation.

Burkhart hesitated as his jaws clinched hard, then he said quietly, "No. But I think someday she'll be engaged to the county sheriff. Or at least—to somebody like him."

"You say she is a beauty?" continued McWilliams, sensing something unusual in the tone of Burkhart's answers.

"Yes, she's pretty. But it's none of my concern anymore."

Glancing at Burkhart's drawn expression, McWilliams asked cautiously, "This lack of concern—a recent development, is it?"

"It doesn't matter. Some things just don't work out. That's all."

"Now, don't give her up yet, Jason. Maybe you shouldn't burn any bridges until you're sure about things."

"I'm sure enough of one thing," answered Burkhart firmly. "If we—if she's associated with me in any way, she'll be in danger. She shouldn't even come near me.

"Do you remember what almost happened to that navy captain's wife, the guy that gave the command to shoot down that Iranian airliner a few years back?"

"Not really, though I do recall something about it."

"She was almost blown up in a car bomb. Her husband was hidden away because the Iranian fanatics marked him for death, but they went after her, too. In Iraq, they have a tradition of killing the nearest relatives of their enemies. If anyone thinks she means something to me, she could get—hurt."

"Does she know how you feel about her?"

"Mac, I'm not even sure I know," answered Burkhart unconvincingly, then, as if speaking to himself, continued, "We just met last week. The night before I flew to New Mexico, we had dinner. Afterwards we walked together—and talked—and towards the end—"

As Burkhart's words faded away, McWilliams glanced across the cab. "Do I at least get to meet her?"

"Only if you bump into her," answered Burkhart, as he gazed out the window at the sunrise. "We're not going out of our way to meet anybody."

Forty miles to the right of the slow-moving pickup, the Diamond Mountains shielded the rising sun from the desert floor, while a second, smaller range a few miles to the west already reflected the rays of the coming day. Just ahead, a kangaroo rat bounded across the hard, packed sand, heading for its burrow, as a light breeze lifted a wisp of dust behind it.

"This our left turn?" asked McWilliams, breaking the silence of the last few minutes.

"Yeah, we're on our last leg. Bed's going to feel good tonight."

"How's the arm doin'?"

Lifting his left arm slightly, Burkhart flinched. "Stiff and sore, but not as painful. The wounds are clean and shallow. At this altitude, they'll heal in a hurry."

"How high are we?"

"Right now, we're at sixty-five hundred feet. The ranch is sixty-seven where it sits."

"Sixty-seven!" exclaimed McWilliams. "You gotta be kiddin' me."

"It's deceiving, alright. Most people think of this desert as being sea level, or below, but this is high desert. It gets hot in the daytime and cold at night."

"I guess winters must be—" McWilliams stopped in mid-sentence as he rolled down his window and squinted at something to his left. "That pile of rocks out there looks out of place, almost like an old building, or corral, or somethin'."

Pointing out the stone ruins and beyond, Burkhart said, "That's where the Pony Express used to run. That was the Dry Creek station. You can still see the trail going around it and through that low area just beyond."

"You don't say," said McWilliams, obviously impressed. "Where does it go from here? I mean, is there anymore of the trail left?"

"It's all there. Goes on for miles, but from here it goes near the house and up over that saddle you see just ahead of us. I believe the Pony Express Trail goes all the way to the California border, and then some."

"You mean it's been just sittin' there all these years?"

"A few people use it for riding, but that's a rarity. But for us, it's our road over to the range behind those hills. We'll use it all the time."

"Now that's truly amazin'. Right here on the ranch, too."

Suddenly, a round of painfully anxious howls reverberated through the open window, quickly followed by a series of high-pitched barks.

Smiling broadly at the near musical greeting, Burkhart sat up eagerly. "That's my dog, Trouble. He knows the sound of the truck, and he's on his way."

In a matter of seconds, the black and tan hound charged out of the sage, fifty yards ahead of the pickup and racing towards it. McWilliams stepped on the break as Burkhart opened his door and shouted, "Good boy, Trouble. Come on, boy!"

Trouble veered instantly at the sound of Jason's voice. Running underneath the door, he slid to a stop, then hopped onto his master's lap and lunged for his face with a joyfully active tongue.

Dodging the wet welcome the best he could, Burkhart laughed out loud, while he fended off Trouble's advances with one hand and vigorously petted him with the other.

McWilliams laughed as well. "Seems a friendly sort. He always this happy to see you?"

"Not exactly," chuckled Burkhart. "I haven't left him for this long since before—in over a year. We're what you call close friends."

"I hope to tell ya!" agreed McWilliams, as he again started down the road. Burkhart shoved Trouble onto the seat between them.

"Trouble, this is Mac. Say hello to a new friend."

As if he understood, the dog bent his head back around his shoulder and sniffed suspiciously. After a short pause, he broke into what resembled a grin, and began to pant contentedly. With a long second look at McWilliams, he sat upright in the seat, leaned into Burkhart's side, and eagerly turned his interest to what lay ahead.

"That was easy enough," said McWilliams.

"He's a good judge of character, that's all. He's a good watchdog, but like I said before, he doesn't know cows."

McWilliams put out his hand for Trouble to smell, then patted him on the head. "Well, for now, we don't need no cow dog. A watchdog'll do just fine."

As the pickup pulled up to the front porch, a blazing rim of sunlight crested the horizon, tinting the desert with yellow-orange iridescence. From the hills beyond the house, a blanket of cold air drifted past, and somewhere hidden in the long shadows, a pair of quail signaled back and forth.

After stepping out of the cramped cab, Burkhart threw his good arm towards the barn, "You can stow your saddle in there," he said, then went to the screen door, and opened it. "I'll get some breakfast going, and you can have a look around."

In the small kitchen, Trouble found his familiar corner by the stove as Burkhart lit two burners and covered the flames with the coffee pot and a cast iron skillet. In the skillet, he dropped several slices of cured bacon, then took a can of beans down and opened it.

A moment later, McWilliams returned from the barn; after taking one look at the stove-top, he jerked to a stop and raised a bushy gray eyebrow. "Seems to me you know more about ranchin' than you let on," he jested. "That's a real cowboy's breakfast you got goin' there."

Burkhart shrugged, "Now, I never said I could cook. Besides, it's quick, and we're low on supplies."

"Uh-huh," grumbled Mac, as he peered into the skillet and the cold can of beans. "Well, Boss, if it's all the same to you, I'd like to volunteer to make up the grocery list when we go to town."

"Only if you volunteer to do the cooking, too."

"Deal!" answered McWilliams emphatically, then crossed the kitchen floor to poke his head through an open door. "Two bedrooms?"

"Yeah. That's about it," replied Burkhart apologetically. "There's an outhouse out back, and I'm afraid it's not for decoration, either. This place was built a while back."

"Aw, it'll be just like home," chirped McWilliams. "It's like it was when I was growin' up. We got all the essentials we need to start up."

While the bacon sizzled and popped, Burkhart turned it occasionally and kept an eye on McWilliams, who moved from window to window, pausing in front of each before going to the next.

"Got a good view from the house," he commented matter-of-factly. "I also noticed the house sits on high ground."

After forking several strips of shriveled bacon and scraping them onto a plate, Burkhart replied, "You can see the road for about a mile before it disappears behind the knolls. The hills in back of us are about three hundred yards away, and they lead into nothing but rough country." After dumping the beans in the skillet and giving them a stir, he added grimly, “If they come, they’ll have to come from the road, the same way we came in.”

McWilliams turned uneasily. “I didn’t really want to bring it up so soon, but—”

“It’s alright, Mac. It’s there, staring us in the face, whether we talk about it or not. There’s no need to beat around the bush. We either take it head on, or not at all.”

“Good!” agreed McWilliams heartily. “I’m glad that’s cleared up. Pussy-footin’ around never was my style, neither.”

The beans and bacon vanished quickly, but the two men lingered at the table, both nursing a second cup of black coffee. Glancing around the house, McWilliams grew curious. “Where do you keep your valuables? I don’t see a place for them.”

Picking up his cup, Burkhart stood. “Over here,” he said, motioning for McWilliams to follow, then went out to the porch.

Just to the right of the doorway, he moved a chair to one side and knelt down. With a pocketknife, he eased up the plank, then grabbed the edge with a fingertip and removed it. Beneath it was a long metal box, resembling a steel suitcase. Lifting it through the space, Burkhart set it down heavily.

“This hasn’t got a lock,” he said, releasing two snap hinges, “but it’s waterproof when it’s closed up tight.”

Lying open on the floor, the case held a photo album, camera, and a few assorted boxes in the upper level, while in the lower was a set of binoculars, a lever-action rifle, pump shotgun, and a pistol. All showed signs of heavy use.

“What we have here,” began Burkhart, as he lifted the rifle, “is a 30-30 Winchester, and that pistol is a second generation Colt .45 that belonged to my grandfather.”

McWilliams picked up the shotgun and looked it over carefully. “Where’d you get this ‘un?”

“That came with the ranch. The previous owner threw it ‘in to boot.’”

Opening the slide action with a crisp snap, McWilliams examined the chamber. "They had some of these around in my war and the one before that, too. But come to think of it, I heard somewhere's these did some time in Iraq, in that house to house fightin'."

"Well, that one you're holding could have been in all three places. It was made in 1901, and the barrel has been cut down to twenty inches. It holds seven rounds of double aught buck in the tube, plus one in the chamber."

McWilliams brow wrinkled. "Loaded up, this'll make a mean weapon. Mind if I take charge of this one?"

"Not at all. I feel better with a rifle and pistol, myself," answered Burkhart as he removed the Colt and a box of shells. "I know where the 30-30 hits up to three hundred yards, and the pistol to one hundred. Up close, it gets even better."

"How're we set for ammunition?"

"We're low," answered Burkhart anxiously. "That's number one on the list when we hit town. They'll likely have plenty of rifle shells, but the .45s and the double aught will be scarce. There's not much call for those out here, but we can get some in a week if we order them at the hardware store."

"Do we keep the guns out?" asked McWilliams, with a glint in his eye.

"Keeping guns packed away is like keeping a guard dog on a leash," said Burkhart as he handed up a box of shells. "By the time you're able to get to your weapons—there's likely to be no point."

McWilliams nodded sternly. "I like a practical man—and a cautious one."

After removing the pistol and two boxes of cartridges, Burkhart lowered the case and replaced the board. "Anymore coffee for you, Mac?"

"Nope. Bed sounds better."

"Me, too. You take the first room off the kitchen. There's sheets and such folded on the bed."

McWilliams started for the room, carrying the shotgun and shells, then stopped suddenly and turned. “Say, Boss, you think we could get a hold of some black powder for my pistols? We may have need of them again.”

For a moment, Burkhart’s face went blank. Racing through his mind was the scorching flash of gunpowder and eyes stretched wide with shock—a human life slipping away as he used a man for a shield against a storm of bullets. For an instant, he smelled the smoke, heard the screams, and saw the pilot go down.

Forcing the picture from his mind, Burkhart responded, “I’m sure we can get what we need. We can always use the added fire power.”

“Maybe we can buy some automatics,” added McWilliams. “Semis, I mean. Then we’d really have an arsenal.”

Burkhart shook his head. “I don’t think we should try and buy anything, unless we can buy it privately. They trace everything nowadays, and we don’t need our names showing up in anyone’s computer system. We’ll have to make do with what we have, and if you ask me, we’ve got plenty, right here.”

CHAPTER EIGHT

His left arm had swollen and grown more stiff during the few hours Burkhart had slept, and the pain woke him shortly after one o'clock in the afternoon. He decided to let McWilliams sleep, and after changing into a fresh long-sleeve shirt, lifted his hat from the rack and stepped outside.

The scorching midday sun blanched the vivid colors of morning, but the air temperature was still tolerable. Standing in the shade of the porch, Burkhart leaned a heavily muscled shoulder against one of its posts and surveyed the scene in front of him. Immediately to his left was the corral and barn he had worked on for so many hours, the first weeks he had arrived. In the distance was the long string of posts he had been setting for over a month. Below his feet were the steps he had repaired—the place he and Kimberly had last sat together.

What was she going to think when he ignored her, when he did what he must to protect her? Would she think of him as just another city misfit? Or would she forget about him all together and continue her life as if he never existed? As Jason Burkhart thought of Kimberly and the repugnant Sheriff Muller, he felt his stomach sour, yet knew he could do nothing to interfere. At present, everything he desired for himself—everything he had planned for—must be suspended indefinitely. When it came to Kimberly Whitney, there would be neither hope nor hopelessness. There was nothing left but to accept his fate. For now, all he could do was exist in the fog of the unknowable.

He glanced down at his brown, callused hands—hands that he would not have recognized a year earlier. A year? Had it been only one year since the relentless pain had driven him into the isolation of Nevada's high desert? And was it only three months ago, trying to escape the memories of the past, that he had moved onto the ranch? Time was such a relative thing, and easily warped by despair—or exhilaration.

For so long, the days had passed at a tortuously slow pace, as if the desert, or his own grief, had slowed the passing of each and every minute. Yet it was barely a week ago, in the midst of what he thought of as wasteland, he found himself among moonlit roses, walking with a beautiful woman he had not even known the day before. But most incredible of all, the nightmarish vision of a smoke-filled airliner, strewn with the dead and dying, seemed a very distant memory. But that catastrophic event was only a few hours old.

Now the bizarre cycle was starting all over. Again, he was retreating into the seclusion of the desert, once more grasping at the faintest chance that solitude would shield him from the tragedies of his past. But this time, the foe that stalked him was a tangible one, an enemy he could fight. And for that, at least, he was grateful.

Breaking into his thoughts was the banging of the back door as it slammed shut amidst a blistering array of swearing and the rapid approach of boot heels.

Bursting out the front door was McWilliams. "Know what we gotta do first to this place?" he roared, still tucking his shirttail into his pants.

"What's that?" asked Burkhart, startled at Mac's flushed appearance.

"Finish off the foundation of the 'john.' I came out of it just as a four-foot buzz-tail slid between my legs! Might have got real acquainted, but for me jumpin' half outta my skin."

"They're around, alright," grinned Burkhart. "I've been thinning them out as I burn the old brush piles and carry off the junk. These rattlesnakes can't take the sun this time of day and start heading for shade. It can be rough around here, sometimes. Seems like nearly everything in this desert country either bites, sticks, or stings."

"But I thought you liked it out here."

"It suits me just fine, Mac. I've never been anywhere, or heard of any place that doesn't have drawbacks. If a person understands this desert and accepts it for what it is, instead of fighting it, he can have a good life here. And there's beauty in this land, as well as freedom. As far as I'm concerned, this is untamed country and still part of the old frontier."

"Well you're right about that," replied McWilliams, as his color returned. "When we get into the cattle business, you'll really see how little things have changed in the last hundred years. There's open range to be worked and horses to do it on, brands to be fired, fences to mend, feed to be stored, and a hundred other things that still have to be done the old way—includin' getting' rid of them snakes."

"You'll find me all ears and a good student, Mac," offered Burkhart, with a distant tone to his voice. "Are you ready to go to town?"

"Yep. Want me to drive again?"

"No, I need to loosen up the arm a little and work some of the stiffness out."

"What do we do when we get there?" questioned McWilliams, as the two headed for the Willys. "I mean, how do we handle me bein' with you?"

Burkhart opened the truck door, then paused, rubbing his eyes against the glare. "Let's see—no last names, for one thing."

"Don't they know yours by now?"

"No. I've never told most of them. The sheriff knows, and Ms. Whitney knows, but that's about it. I pay cash for everything and don't socialize much. And like I said, I've only been here three months. I haven't even bothered to get a mailbox, yet."

Mac scratched his stubbled chin thoughtfully. "Well now, that's a big break in our favor. You don't use a bank, you say?"

"Not anymore, at least not lately. I've been—" Burkhart broke into an ironic smile. "I've been trying to keep my life as simple as possible."

Catching the spirit of the moment, McWilliams scoffed, "Simple! You're lookin' down a dry well on that regard! I'd hate to see things if you liked your life complicated."

As Burkhart and McWilliams entered through the open door of the hardware store, Giz sat at his desk behind the counter, facing the wall. With his nose wrinkled in concentration, he clumsily shuffled through a stack of invoices. "Be with you in a minute," he mumbled, taking a quick glance over his shoulder. "Oh, hello," he said, then leaned back in his wooden swivel chair, "how was your trip to New Mexico?"

"Good," replied Burkhart casually. "I brought back a foreman. Giz, this is Travis."

"You a cattleman?" asked Giz, as the two men shook hands.

"Long as I can remember," smiled McWilliams.

"Aren't you going to introduce me?" added a feminine voice from out of nowhere.

Burkhart turned slowly, feeling his face grow suddenly hot from the pounding of his chest. "Kimberly!" he said guardedly. "How are you?"

"Fine," answered Kimberly, with a wisp of a smile. "Did you buy any cattle? We were talking about that before you left."

"Ah, no, I didn't," replied Burkhart, unable to resist looking into her cordial brown eyes. Then, fighting a wave of nausea, he tried to continue. "I didn't—I mean—I don't—"

"He got me instead, ma'am," interrupted McWilliams quickly. "My name's Travis, recently from the Bar MT, out of New Mexico."

"Yes," agreed Burkhart, regaining his composure. "He's my new foreman."

"No, ma'am," grinned McWilliams. "Right now, just a hired hand. When we get our livestock, then I'll be foreman."

"Call me Kimberly. It's nice to meet you. I've heard of the MT."

"Sure enough?" chimed McWilliams, obviously pleased. "And you must be that lady rancher I've heard so much about."

Before the conversation could continue, Burkhart took a piece of paper from his shirt pocket, then said abruptly, "You'll have to excuse me, Kimberly. I have quite a bit of things to order. Giz, could you help me in the back?"

As Giz and Burkhart walked away, McWilliams watched the bright face of the young woman cloud with confusion and surprise. "He's got quite a bit on his mind lately," he said apologetically. "There's some things he has to do, now that he's back, that are going to keep him mighty busy. For a while, he won't have much time to spend with anybody. That is, anybody in particular."

"I see," replied Kimberly, her expression tightening.

"Begging your pardon, Miss Kimberly," countered McWilliams, but with softness in his voice, "but no, you don't see. There's things that can't be explained that call the shots right now, but he's a good man. One of the few I've ever met. One to believe in—and wait for."

Kimberly stared at McWilliams. "I don't understand. What are you trying to say?"

McWilliams paused, searching for words, then said, "Stay away from him, Kimberly. But don't go away."

Before she could ask another question, McWilliams turned and followed Burkhart to the back of the store, passing Giz on the way.

"Forgot my pencil," said Giz, as he went behind the counter. Peering at the two men at the rear of the store, he asked, "What do you suppose that was all about? Sounds like he's got some serious problems."

"What?" asked Kimberly, still distracted by the sudden turn of events.

"Anybody that'd walk away from you without being told to has got to have something important on his mind."

"I don't know about that," replied Kimberly weakly. "But he does have his work cut out for him getting that ranch back into shape. I'm glad he'll have some help."

"I better go see what he needs," moaned Giz. Shoving the pencil behind his ear, he reached into his shirt pocket for a handful of sunflower seeds. "Did you need anything?"

"No. I just came in to—no, I don't," she answered, purposefully avoiding the inquisitive gaze of the storeowner. "I'll see you later."

Cracking a sunflower seed between his yellowed teeth, Giz thoughtfully watched Kimberly leave, then worked his way down the aisle, spitting the shells onto the wooden floor as he went. "Oh, she likes him, alright," he muttered to himself. Then, looking towards the two men, he asked, "What can I do for you today?"

"Let's see," replied Burkhart, unfolding a small piece of paper. "How about a mile of electric fence wire and a—Oh, before I get going, I want you to know that Travis here will be doing most of the buying from now on. I'll be spending more time on the ranch."

"That's fine. You want some electric fence wire, and what else?"

"Fifty pounds of dog food, three or four boxes of 30-30 shells, three boxes of 12-gauge, double aught buckshot and .45 long Colts, if you have any. And we'll need to order some black powder and percussion caps, too. And a half-dozen quart canteens."

Giz put another sunflower seed in his heavy jaws as his brow furrowed. "You going hunting?"

"We like to target shoot," said Burkhart evenly. "There's not much to do out at the ranch for entertainment."

Giz nodded apathetically. "Don't have any .45s, but I've got black powder and caps in stock. Some of the deer hunters around here are starting to use that old-time stuff. I don't care for it, myself. Not enough killing power for me."

"Can you order me some .45s? Say four boxes?"

"Sure. I only got one box of buckshot, but I got three boxes of 30-30. Lot of folk shoot that caliber around here, but it'll take a week or more to get more buckshot and the.45s. Anything else?"

Burkhart hesitated, but decided to take a chance. "How does a person go about getting some dynamite?"

Seemingly unsurprised by the question, Giz asked lazily, "Gonna do some mining?"

"No, just the opposite," returned Burkhart in a relaxed tone. "There's a shaft on my place I want to close up. I can't afford to lose any cows in it."

Giz nodded. "I'll think about it," he said, rubbing his chin, then added quickly, "I'll get back to you. I think I know how I can get around some of the red tape and permits."

McWilliams started for the cash register with the canteens, then looked across the highway at Digger's gas station. In front of it was a newspaper box. As Burkhart went with Giz to pay the bill and pick up the shells, McWilliams went outside, dropped the canteens in the bed of the pickup, then headed for Digger's.

Sliding the glass door of the ammunition cabinet open from the rear, Giz reached for the shells and black powder. "That trip to those ranches down in New Mexico—did it turn out like you wanted?"

"It did. I learned a lot, and what I missed, Travis can fill me in on."

Handing over the shells, Giz Gibson paused, almost imperceptibly. "Didn't you say you were going to fly out of San Francisco to get down there?"

Burkhart glanced anxiously over his shoulder as he pulled a roll of bills from his pants pocket, but McWilliams was not in sight. Then, paying Gibson, he said, "I took a bus part of the way, but I did end up coming back through San Francisco."

The cash register rang, and the door rolled out, jerking to a noisy stop. "Did you hear about that shoot-out with those sand-jockeys? That was a hell of a thing, wasn't it?"

Pretending to wipe something from his eye, Burkhart tried to sound disinterested. "I heard about it, but I've been too busy to keep up with it."

Palming a handful of change to Burkhart, Gibson continued peevishly. "Aw, it's gotten crazy. Somebody gives them Arabs what they deserve, and the next thing you know, they're trying to arrest him. Turns out, all of them Muslims but one had Mexican names on their driver's licenses and likely crossed over from Mexico. But one of the sons-a-bitches was a U.S. citizen. Now the stinking ACLU is sticking their nose into the fracas, saying our guy violated his civil rights. It's disgusting! But if they can do it to Ollie North, they can do it to anybody!"

Burkhart stalled, not knowing how to respond, then, hearing a familiar step behind him, turned to see McWilliams, white-faced, standing in the doorway. "Time's a-wastin', Boss," he said, with an artificial smile. "We better be headin' out."

"Sure is," answered Burkhart heartily, then waved at Giz. "We'll be back in a week or so for the rest of the order, and hopefully, that dynamite. Take it easy."

Once inside the cab, Burkhart started the engine and took a second to look at McWilliams, who was unfolding a newspaper. "This paper of theirs got here early today. I ain't read it yet, but look here!"

Under the headline DEATH TOLL CLIMBS AT S.F. AIRPORT was a composite sketch of the man wanted by the San Francisco police department. The shape of the jaw was wrong, the mouth was not his, but someone had vividly remembered his eyes.

"Look familiar?" asked McWilliams nervously.

"It could be anybody," assured Burkhart, somewhat relieved by the poor rendering.

"I don't know, Jason. It's too close for comfort if you ask me."

"You know it's me, Mac, so you see the likeness. For anyone else, it's just some unlucky man running from two governments."

Holding the sketch at arm's length as Burkhart pulled out onto Main Street, McWilliams cocked his head to the left, then to the right, studying what he saw. "Maybe you're right at that," he agreed, then laid the paper in his lap. Using his finger as a pointer, he began reading the lead story. A short moment later, he stopped and slowly raised his eyes. "Afraid there's bad news, Jason."

"How bad?"

"The pilot—he died last night."

Visibly stunned, Burkhart sank despondently into his seat. After a long silence, he said soberly, "I hoped—I hoped to God he would make it. Is there anything about his family—any children?"

McWilliams shook his head gravely. "No, nothin'. But it does say it was the terrorists that shot him. They make it real clear it wasn't you."

"That doesn't make a whole lot of difference now."

"No. No, it don't make a whole bunch of difference now. It is a terrible thing that he's dead, but the fact is, he was a casualty in what amounted to small war. People forget, all too quick and easy, how bad it gets in a war. And you know now, like you knew then, it could'a been a lot worse than just the pilot. What you did on that plane doesn't come under the headin' of good or bad, right or wrong. It's just what had to be done under the circumstances. Just like in war. There was no other way but the way you took."

Burkhart sighed wearily. "I know, Mac. I keep going over it in my mind, and I know I had no choice. But still, it can drive you crazy. If only he could have lived."

"Wanta know what else is here or wait 'till later?"

"Go ahead, I'm alright," replied Burkhart, sliding more upright. "Go on."

"Says here that the San Francisco police are sayin' the FBI is claiming national security reasons and ain't cooperating with them in their manhunt, and so far, there's been no federal warrant issued. But the city lawyers are trying to—what they call—'formalize' one in Superior Court for 'unlawful flight to avoid prosecution, manslaughter, and public endangerment, whatever all that means."

"What that means, so far anyway, is the FBI hasn't filed criminal charges against me, and the Superior Court judge wants to know why."

McWilliams tapped his finger on the paper. "That Agent Mader. He's on our side, I'll bet ya. I figured him that way."

"I hope you're right, Mac. This will never work without some help from somewhere.

"Well, there's one other piece of good news here."

"I could use some. What is it?"

"You know that bastard shrink I told you about? That Webb fella? He was the one we saw on that newscast back at that diner in California."

"Yeah."

"He kept calling you Burthark at the airport. And now that's how the papers have it. Just Berthark. I guess he couldn't recollect your first name, either. And he spelled it B-e-r-t-h-a-r-k. It could even be read as Berth—ark. That'll throw 'em off!"

Jason nodded. "If Agent Mader wants, he could get hold of all the airport records and hold that information. Maybe he and I could, I don't know—work something out. A pardon, maybe."

Scratching the side of his head, McWilliams agreed, "I think you're on to something there. It sounds possible. Maybe one of them presidential pardons."

Stopping in front of a small market, McWilliams got out and walked to the driver's side of the pickup. "Buy whatever you think we need," advised Burkhart. "I'm going back to Digger's, fill up with gas, and pick up a few more things. I'll pick you up in about ten minutes."

"You got any preferences for what to eat?"

"You're the cook now," said Burkhart, as he pulled away. "You decide. I can eat anything that isn't moving."

The two-pump service station was in the middle of town, yet looked all but abandoned. Out front was a chair, a coke machine, and a newspaper stand, but despite its appearance, the station served as the unofficial information center for the entire county. As Burkhart rolled to a stop under the weather-beaten awning, Digger Mosby sat outside in a battered oak chair, balancing himself against the wall on its back two legs.

"How was the trip?" asked Mosby, his feet still dangling in the air.

"I cut it short, but it turned out fine," offered Burkhart, as he turned on the pump and began filling the tank. "Hired a man named Travis to help out. He'll be doing quite a bit of my trading in town for me."

"Have much experience with cows?"

"Forty years of it."

"Ought to be enough," said Digger approvingly.

"You know, Digger, what he's going to need, that I don't have, though, is some good maps of that country there in back of the ranch. I heard you might have some blow ups of that whole area."

"You heard right," replied Mosby, bringing his chair to rest on all four legs. "I'll see what I got."

Burkhart had finished off the tank and started on the Jeep can on the sideboard of the Willys when Mosby returned with an armful of rolled maps.

"Got just the thing," he said eagerly, and began unrolling the large sheets on the hood of the pickup.

"These show close to three hundred square miles of backcountry and rangeland up that way. He can't get lost with these here."

"You been through much of that area yourself?" asked Burkhart, as he replaced the gas nozzle on the old pump and started for the front of the truck.

"Years back. But, yeah. I know that country."

Studying the maps for a moment, Burkhart took one, spread it out carefully, then put his finger down on a tiny symbol. "What is that?"

"Well, now," began Digger, reaching for his glasses. "Let me get my cheaters on, and I'll tell ya."

"And this one here, too," added Burkhart, pointing to a second figure.

"That one there is a mine. This country's full of 'em, so you need to be careful where you step. This thing here stands for a spring, but it's been a bad year for snowfall in the mountains. I doubt there'll be much water this time of year. It gets dry as hell out there, and just about as hot."

"These will do just fine, Digger. What do I owe you for them and the gas?"

"Oh, no need to pay for the maps, I got plenty. But you can pay for the gas. That I run short of, now and then."

"Thanks, Digger," said Burkhart, handing him fifty dollars. "Keep the change."

Digger glanced at the bills and smiled respectfully. "Fair enough, Jason, fair enough. By the way, did you see Kimberly yet? She saw you drive by a while back, when she was here getting gas. The way she watched you go up the street— I figured she would look you up."

"Yes. I saw her, already," replied Burkhart nonchalantly.

Digger folded his glasses and dropped them into his shirt pocket, grinning broadly. "Ol' Bob's got hisself some competition, eh?"

Burkhart flinched at the suggestion, but remained cool. "No. He's got nothing to worry about from me," he said, sliding into the cab. "I'm not interested in anything of his."

Digger Mosby's gray eyes rolled open, as his head turned sharply on a skinny neck. "That so?" he questioned, but the starting of the pickup drowned his words. As Burkhart waved a hasty goodbye and drove onto the street, he croaked in disbelief, "Is that so, now?"

Mac was standing outside the grocery store with four bulging cardboard boxes at his feet when Burkhart stopped in front of him. As they loaded the food onto the bed, a white patrol car approached slowly from the rear. Coming within inches of the side of the pickup, the officer inside cast an insolent sneer at Burkhart.

After the car had rolled on past, McWilliams stared angrily. "What in blue blazes was that all about? Was he lookin' for somethin' in particular?"

"He's hoping for trouble. But he's wasting his time."

"Who was it, anyway?"

Setting down the last box in the truck bed and giving it a hard shove, Burkhart slammed the tailgate and latched the chains. "Remember your foreman back in New Mexico?"

"Yeah."

"He reminded me a lot of this fella. That was the county sheriff."

Mac frowned worriedly. "What's he got against you?"

"He wanted the ranch I bought, I think," reflected Burkhart, then paused. "And he doesn't want me around Kimberly. Like I told you, he wants to marry her."

Opening the passenger door, McWilliams glanced at Burkhart sympathetically, but said nothing until both were inside. "You know, Jason," he said, looking straight ahead, "words don't mean as much as they used to. We're hit with 'em from all sides by radio and television, newspapers, magazines, and such. Some words just naturally lose their meanin' from being overused and worn out, sort of. You're in some hard times right now. Real hard. And I know what it's like because my wife died of the cancer—and it was slow.

"What you have to do now, and for maybe a couple of years, is to brace yourself and endure it. Endurance is the word, Jason, bare bone, ugly endurance, until it's finally over. There's no short cut across hard times."

After a moment of silence, Burkhart's eyes hardened. "Well said, Travis, and thanks. There's a long way yet to go, and it's going to get worse before there is any chance at all of it getting better."

"You're up to it. You got what it takes, Boss. I know it."

Burkhart nodded and forced a smile. "Are you getting hungry? I'd like to eat in town one last time, since it may be a while until I get back in."

"Sure thing," replied Mac cheerily. "You're gonna be eatin' my cookin' for a good while. I guess you're entitled to one last wish."

CHAPTER NINE

"The best place in town to eat is the International Hotel," explained Jason, as he drove down Main Street. It's just up a little ways, but we'll drive and park out front, so we can keep an eye on the supplies."

A short distance across the highway, and half a block to the west, Burkhart stopped in front of the two-story wooden building. As he got out and started for the boardwalk, he pointed to a historical plaque on the outside wall.

"This place was first built in Virginia City and later rebuilt here in 1863, during a silver strike. It used to be a good hotel in its day, but now it more or less survives as a café. But the food's good."

Mac glanced at the plaque, then at the white posts that held up a long balcony. On the lower story was a door with BAR written above it, and another further down, with CAFÉ.

"Looks like it was a nice place in its day," remarked McWilliams, as they entered the dining room.

Except for a single waitress, the room was deserted, and Burkhart took the booth nearest the far wall, next to the window. He had shared the same table with Matty and Kimberly only the week before. Smiling at the young, but exceptionally thin woman, Burkhart said, "Doris not working today?"

"She comes in later," answered the waitress lethargically. "I'm on till six tonight. You want a menu?"

"Yes, please. We're having an early dinner."

Walking slowly to their table, the woman laid menus down in what seemed like slow motion, then asked, "You live 'round here?"

"A ways out of town, east of here," answered Burkhart, noticing the gaunt-looking face. "I've been here for three months."

"Thought I recognized you," she said to Burkhart, then looked at McWilliams. "You ready to order?"

"Two coffees to start with, and then we'll be ready."

Watching the waitress plod away, McWilliams raised an eyebrow. "Who's that?"

"I don't know her. Someone else is usually here when I come in. But there are quite a few people like her—that cause you to wonder. Refugees, maybe, from some other place, that have come to the desert to escape their troubles or their past, or both. In the vastness and simplicity of this country, a person's problems have a way of shrinking. Nothing changes much out here, either. That provides a sense of security and natural comfort, because a person knows what to expect from day to day. We're isolated and insulated. Life is simple."

Mac studied Burkhart's face for a moment, then started to ask a question, but thinking better of it, said instead, "Maybe more folks oughta try it. It seems a good way to handle things and get a fresh start. Lots of people could use some time to let the dust settle in their lives, before goin' on with it."

Returning with the coffee and mugs, the waitress offered, "My name's Ella. There's a newspaper on the counter, if you want to read it. It's today's paper."

"We bought one already," returned Mac. "Thank you just the same."

Methodically filling their cups, Ella continued speaking slowly. "Then you saw the picture of the fella that shot those Arabs over in California. He's sure caused a commotion doing that. But I don't think he did anything bad. They should leave him alone."

Burkhart nodded. "Maybe they won't find him, Ella. Maybe he can hide out somewhere."

The corners of her thin lips turned upward, and her dull eyes brightened. "I would like that. I would like that a lot. I hope they never find him!"

After taking their orders, Ella disappeared into the kitchen. As they waited for their meal, several other locals drifted in and took seats along the counter. Some of the faces Burkhart recognized. Most were new to him, but each obviously knew the other. Engaging in idle conversation that sounded almost artificial, they seemed unaware that anyone else was in the room.

For ten minutes, Burkhart and McWilliams listened quietly, but no mention of the shooting came up, nor did anyone show interest in the folded newspaper. But as Ella emerged from the kitchen with two plates of food, the light coming through the glass front door dimmed before swinging open.

First to appear was Kimberly, then, dressed in street clothes, the sheriff stepped heavily onto the plank floor. Calling those along the counter by name, Kimberly greeted each with a smile as the sheriff impatiently stood behind her, doling out nods.

Ella clumsily set the food down in front of Burkhart and McWilliams, and without speaking, started back to the counter. "Hi, Kimberly," Ella said warmly, then dropped her eyes. "Hello, Sheriff Muller. There's a paper on the counter, if you two want to read it. It came early."

"Thanks, Ella," returned Kimberly, catching sight of Burkhart. As Muller's large hand came to rest on her shoulder, she averted her eyes and casually picked up the paper. "Let's sit over there, Bob," she said, indicating the table furthest from Burkhart's corner.

With teeth clinched tight, Burkhart watched Kimberly and Bob Muller cross to the other side of the room. He turned his head away, but his attention would not follow. And for an instant, as she took her seat, their eyes met.

Missing nothing, Mac did what he could. "Getting' crowded in here. We best eat and get on our way."

Sitting stone-faced, Burkhart made no reply. Glaring at the hulking figure sitting next to Kimberly, the skin on his face and neck grew increasingly hot. Then, as if feeling the stare, Muller turned and glanced over at Burkhart, seeing him for the first time.

Along with recognition came an arrogant sneer that spread tauntingly into a sadistic smile. Leaning closer to Kimberly's ear, Muller said something, then snickered. Saying nothing, Kimberly nodded solemnly, then unfolded the newspaper and pushed a strand of light brown hair back into place.

"He looks a bit meaner'n old Hogan back at the ranch," commented Mac cautiously. "But you know he'll have to wait."

"What?" asked Burkhart, finally turning towards his plate. "What was that?"

"I said that the sheriff will have to wait. I can see how you're feelin', but you can't let him get in the way of what has to be done."

Taking a deep breath, Burkhart rubbed a hand over his forehead and face. "You're right," he grunted. "Let's eat and get out of here."

Ignoring Muller's excessive laughter and boisterous comments to those at the counter, Burkhart and McWilliams ate in silence, not giving the other table a second look. It was obvious that the sheriff was enjoying himself, but no less than the conceited view he held of his own importance.

Half way through his steak, however, Burkhart lost his appetite and began picking at his food, forcing himself to eat. "I've got to go talk to her," he said, "to cancel our business deal."

"What was it about?"

"She had the calves and breeding stock we need. I was going to buy them from her; we would have shared some of the work. We'll have to get our cattle somewhere else. When I tell her that, she's going to think—"

"She'll think just what she's supposed to," interrupted McWilliams. "And word will get around that you two don't have nothing to do with each other. And all the while, she'll stay clear of you—and be safe like you want."

Burkhart tapped the tabletop with his fork and stared at his plate. A moment later, he reluctantly came to his feet and slowly crossed the floor.

Kimberly put down the paper as Muller snapped, "What do you want?"

Disregarding the sheriff, Burkhart looked deeply into the eyes of Kimberly Whitney, knowing it would likely be his last chance to do so. "I'm sorry, but I've decided not to take you up on that cattle deal we talked about. I'll be going through another party."

Kimberly's eyes filled with surprise, but not allowing her to respond, Burkhart impulsively extended his hand across the table to shake hers. "No hard feelings?"

Before she could react, Muller backhanded Burkhart's arm with such force that it crossed his body and slammed into his wounded left forearm, sending a stabbing pain up and through his shoulder. "Get your hand out of my face!" he ordered, then haughtily added, "Kimberly, this guy is such a loser!"

Bringing his right arm back to his side and ignoring the pain in his left, Burkhart waited for Kimberly to reply. He could say virtually nothing to her by way of explanation, but at least he could apologize.

"It seems," she said finally, "that while you were in New Mexico, you changed your mind—about a lot of things."

Jason swallowed hard. "Yes. It would certainly seem so," he said, watching Kimberly's face flush with confusion and embarrassment. "But if you lost buyers on account of me, I will cover any losses."

"You're damned right, you will!" interrupted Muller. "A verbal contract is binding in Nevada. It's not like the big city where you came from."

Kimberly scowled at Muller. “Please, Bob!” she said sternly, then turned to Jason.

As her eyes focused on him, she caught sight of blood soaking through his left shirtsleeve. Recovering her composure, she said, “No harm done, Mr. Burkhart. I’m sorry it didn’t work out for us.”

Jason Burkhart tried to smile, but the ‘Mr.’ stung too much. “So am I,” he said softly, then turned and walked away.

Bob Muller chuckled and pointed at Burkhart with this thumb. “What a jerk.”

Dismissing Muller’s rudeness, Kimberly thought of the blood on Jason’s shirt and casually leaned forward to look at the floor where Jason had stood. A bright red drop marked the spot. Whatever had happened to his arm since he left Nevada was much more than a scratch.

As Burkhart walked back to his table, Kimberly’s eyes followed him. She noticed that after he took his seat, he held his arm under the table, then covered the bloody stain with his right hand. It was as if he were trying to hide it.

Suddenly, Kimberly grabbed the newspaper, her eyes darting rapidly over the story of the shooting, and the reports of the eleventh man being wounded—in the left arm!

Flipping the paper over, Kimberly stared at the composite sketch. At first, there was nothing—then she noticed the eyes.

The sound of a glass shattering commanded the customers’ attention, as ice cubes slid across Kimberly’s table and onto the floor in all directions. Everyone turned and looked. Kimberly sat stunned, her face pale, her eyes wide and fixed on Jason.

Muller’s voice boomed suddenly. “What did you say?”

With no response from Kimberly, Sheriff Muller jerked the paper from her tight grip and stood up as he studied the sketch on the front page. For a long moment, only the crinkling of the paper broke the tense silence as

Muller scanned the story about the highjacking. Then slowly, he raised his head and looked straight at Burkhart. But now he looked at him as he had never looked before.

His cockiness gone, and his assurance shaken, his eyes narrowed with doubt. "It's hard to believe, but you may be right," he mumbled to himself. "Berthark could be Burkhart. Dark hair, six feet, one eighty, and early to mid-thirties."

"How do you know his last name?" asked Kimberly nervously. "He's told no one in town."

"I told you I've pulled him over a bunch of times, didn't I? It's on his driver's license."

"But the article says Berthark," stammered Kimberly, vainly trying to repair the damage she had done. "And the picture doesn't even look like him."

His expression growing more sinister, the sheriff replied, "You're the one that saw the resemblance, Kimberly, not me!"

Sauntering over to Burkhart, he tossed the paper onto the table, pointing a big finger at the sketch. "It's you, isn't it—Berthark. You're the one they're looking for!"

Kimberly looked painfully at Jason, afraid to hear the answer, yet knowing what it would be.

The few seconds it had taken Muller to make up his mind had given Burkhart time to recover from the initial shock of Kimberly's discovery. With his face void of expression, he glanced at McWilliams, who continued to eat uninterrupted and showed only a casual interest in the paper.

Spinning the paper around, Burkhart pretended to read the caption beneath the sketch as his mind raced for a reply. Stalling more, he took a sip of coffee, then said blandly, "Well, if it's me they're after, the least they could do is not put somebody else's picture in the paper. Besides, Sheriff, there's thousands of Bertharks and thousands of Burkharts in this world, and I'm sure there are hundreds of Jason Bertharks or Burkharts, too, for that matter. Try looking in a big telephone book sometime—if you ever get to a big city."

With a round of subdued laughter in the background, Muller ripped the paper from Burkhart's hands. Under a freshly shaved face, a pair of massive jaw muscles rippled as Muller's eyes grew vicious. "We'll see who's laughing in a couple of days, when the warrant goes through. They'll fax me a copy, and I'll have you. It all fits too well, Mr. Burkhart!"

Totally ignoring the sheriff, Mac took one last gulp of coffee, and asked spryly, "You ready to go, Boss? I'm full as a tick."

Resisting one last look at Kimberly, Burkhart answered, "Let's go," then stood to leave.

Blocking his way, unsure of what to do next, Muller frowned, "Maybe I should run you in right now."

"Now let's see about that idea," said Burkhart, his veneer of patience wearing thin. "If you arrest me, and I'm not who you think I am, you're going to be hit with a false arrest and harassment suit that will go on for at least a year, and maybe end up costing you your job. Considering how you've been hounding me for the last two months, I think I could make a good case. But if I am the one—the one that just killed five men in a face-to-face gun battle—it might be smart to just get out of my way."

Almost involuntarily, Muller took a step backwards, his hand sweeping down for the pistol that was usually there. Halfway to where his holster would have been, his hand froze with the chilling realization he was out of uniform. "I wouldn't try to leave the area!" blurted the sheriff defiantly. "I'll give you until the warrant comes through NCIC. Until then, I'm holding you under suspicion. Don't leave your ranch for any reason, or I'll haul you in. Don't even think of trying to get off it!"

Everyone but Kimberly watched transfixed, as the two men stood toe to toe, but only McWilliams heard Burkhart's last words. "This is your lucky day, Muller," he said, trying to suppress his rage. It was no use. His face darkened with fury and something wild flashed in his eyes. "You crowd me again, and I'll come at you with everything I've got. I've lost everything I care about in this world. I've got absolutely nothing to lose, and that makes me the most dangerous man you ever met."

The sheriff flinched into a slight crouch, like a snake preparing to strike. With every muscle tight, he stood ready; he wanted to take a swing with his big fists—but he hesitated.

"Go ahead. Try it," taunted Burkhart.

Instead of accepting the challenge, Muller cautiously straightened up. It was over. Jason Burkhart stared at Muller for few more seconds, then stepped by him and out the door.

McWilliams tossed a two-dollar tip on the table and walked over to Kimberly, who sat with her head in her hands. "Nice to see you again, Miss Kimberly," he said politely.

Kimberly raised her head, puzzled by his serenity.

"It was good talking to you earlier," he continued. "I'm glad we had the chance. I hope you remember what I said."

"I'm sorry," pleaded Kimberly. "When I saw the picture—his eyes—I was so shocked. I—I didn't—I didn't know—"

Mac touched her hand gently. "Don't worry about it, 'cause he wouldn't want that," he said, then leisurely crossed the room, taking the stares of a dozen people with him. As he stepped down onto the boardwalk, he saw Giz Gibson hand Burkhart a foot long brown package and give him a quick handshake.

"I said goodbye to Kimberly for you, Jason," offered McWilliams, as he slid into the cab of the Willys. "She was sure pretty upset for spillin' the beans."

Burkhart turned the key, then glanced up at the restaurant. "It wasn't her fault," he said, then paused. "I should know by now to stay out of that place."

Shifting into first gear, Burkhart looked across the cab. "She was upset?"

Mac grinned. "She cares for you, son. She surely does."

A few short blocks east of the hotel, a steep switchback marked the end of town and climbing it kept Burkhart busy shifting gears; the noisy transmission made any conversation pointless. But as they crested Austin Summit, McWilliams was waiting with a question. “What do we do, now that they know?”

“There’s not much we can do, but the situation’s not much different than it was before,” replied Burkhart, easing into a quieter overdrive. “Muller has nothing to go on for now, except a hunch. Maybe it’ll take him a while to find out anything definite. By then—who knows.”

“What d’ya think he’ll do first?”

“Call the police in San Francisco, most likely. He’ll give them my description, tell them what he thinks, and where I am.”

“What then?”

Burkhart’s lips tightened as the last glimmer of hope began to fade from his eyes. “I don’t know.”

McWilliams took off his hat and wiped his forehead. “I keep thinkin’ about that FBI fella, Mader. If he’s still on our side, maybe the sheriff won’t get too far. At least he could be doin’ his best to buy us some time.”

“Maybe so,” muttered Burkhart emptily. “This was all a long shot from the beginning.”

“We could always just up and disappear. It’s a big country. Or we could get into Mexico pretty easy. I know some people down there.”

“No, Mac. The running is over. I’ve been running from my problems for over a year. I’ve had all I can take. If this is all life has for me, then so be it. If they get their warrant, they can come serve it. In the meantime, I’ll be getting ready for the terrorists. And if they get here first, the law will just have to wait in line. But whoever wants me, for whatever reason, will have to come get me. I’m going to my ranch, and I’m going to stay there until it’s over. One way or the other!”

“You mean come get us, don’t you?”

With his eyes riveted on the road, Jason answered, “That’s still up to you, Mac. It’s more than I can ask of anyone to stay, now.”

“You don’t have any askin’ to do,” said McWilliams proudly. “I’m stayin’.”

CHAPTER TEN

Immediately after entering the International Hotel, Giz Gibson knew he had missed something big. Several men were scurrying to the windows, while others hurried past him and out onto the street. In the middle of the room, standing alone and swearing to himself, was the sheriff. The only one left sitting was Kimberly, who, with her elbows braced on the table, covered her face with a pair of trembling hands. Walking to her side, Giz asked, "Are you alright Kimberly? What the hell just happened?"

Taking her hands down, she looked up. "I'm not sure, Giz. I just can't bring myself to believe it. It doesn't seem possible. Not him, not now."

"Not who? What's everybody so excited about?"

Struggling to suppress her emotions, Kimberly said, "Did you see today's paper?"

"Yeah."

"The story about the terrorists in San Francisco. The one involved, was named Berthark, which sounds much like Burkhart."

"Yeah, I remember something about it. What of it?"

"Our Jason—the one we know—is the Berthark they're after. I saw the blood on his arm, then when I looked at the drawing—

"I shouldn't have said anything, but I was so shocked, I couldn't help myself. I blurted it out to Bob—I said it was Jason. It was there, in the eyes of the sketch—it just came out so fast!"

"I don't understand," said Gibson, his heavy brow wrinkling. "You mean you thought Jason looked like this other man or—or are you saying—" Gibson paused for a moment, then his eyes flashed with illumination. "Damn!" he exclaimed in amazement. "You could be right!"

"Oh, don't say that, Giz," pleaded Kimberly. But she knew it was too late. The damage had been done, and it was of her own doing!

Coming towards their table was the sheriff. "What do you know about it, Giz?"

"Maybe not much, Bob. But just today he told me he had come through San Francisco on his way back here. It couldn't have been more'n a few days ago, at the most—maybe even less."

"Like yesterday?" questioned the sheriff hungrily.

"It could all be pure coincidence," said Kimberly. "And the name, it's close, but like Jason said, it's not the same. There must be hundreds of people with those two names in California alone."

"Might be coincidence, alright," agreed Giz. "But if it is him, if he's the one, then we got us a celebrity on our hands."

Bob Muller stiffened. "What do you mean 'celebrity'? They're about to arrest him and put him away!"

"They got to give him a trial first, Bob," replied Gibson coolly. "He may not be found guilty of anything. Besides, the paper said there was no arrest warrant issued yet, and there may be some trouble in getting one real soon. Something to do with the judge."

"Don't worry. They'll get the warrant all right. And when they do, I'll be the one that serves it. And that I'm going to enjoy!"

Kimberly looked sincerely at Bob Muller. "You don't know him well enough to dislike him so much. You two got off to a bad start, and I know about the bad feelings, but you haven't given him much of a chance. This could get serious, Bob. I think you'd better go slow and give him the benefit of the doubt, before you go too far. He's had enough trouble in his life without getting accused of something he didn't do."

"Oh?" growled Muller. "So you know all about his private life now?"

"That's not the point, Bob," returned Kimberly harshly. "Or is it?"

Suddenly Fred and Digger Mosby rushed into the café and over to the table. "We just heard," said Digger excitedly. "Is it true? We got us a real live hero here in Austin?"

"Shut up, Digger," ordered the sheriff. "Nobody invited you here."

Digger bristled as his eyes flickered with a newfound life, then he said boldly, "I can come and go as I please, Sheriff. And anyway, I wasn't talkin' to you."

Muller snorted indignantly, but coming up with no reply, retrieved the newspaper and started reading.

"What about it?" asked Fred, his attention on Giz and Kimberly. "Is he the one? Is it true?"

"We don't really know for sure," answered Gibson. "But a lot of things fit."

Digger whistled in amazement. "Hellfire, Boys! He must be one good shot!"

"That, and mighty lucky!" nodded Fred.

"A lot luckier than the pilot was," broke in Muller smugly. "Your 'hero' managed to get him killed."

"What's that?" asked Fred, turning towards the sheriff.

"Says here the pilot got caught in a crossfire and was shot and died. They'll nail his ass for that."

"Maybe it couldn't be helped," rebutted Digger, already aware of the news. "Maybe there was no other way. Maybe he didn't have a choice."

Muller scoffed derisively. "There's always another way. He just got scared, panicked, and started shooting. It's a wonder he didn't get everybody killed."

Giz tapped his thick fingers on the tabletop. "I don't know," he said thoughtfully. "Somehow, I don't think he's the panicky type. I think he had a plan. Otherwise, he couldn't of got all five before they got him and a whole lot more bystanders."

"Well, no matter what, he's finished around here," declared the sheriff. "They'll take him back to California for trial. That'll be the last you'll see of him."

"You mean if'n he's found guilty, don't you?" objected Digger.

Muller laughed. "Are you kidding? He'll be tried in San Francisco, the most limp-wristed town west of New York City. They don't like violence, they don't like guns, and they especially don't like anybody like him. He'll be a snowball in Hell."

"Who was the fella with him?" asked Fred. "Somebody said he had an old guy with him today."

Gibson shrugged. "Name's Travis. Jason met him in New Mexico. I don't think there was any mention of him in the paper."

Taking a moment to scan more of the article, the sheriff glanced up. "No mention of anyone else. If he's got any part in all of this, it can't be very important."

"Or Jason's not the same person," reiterated Kimberly.

Fred eyed the sheriff carefully and tugged on a dangling earlobe with his bony fingers. "What do you plan to do, Sheriff?"

"I'm going to make some phone calls. It won't take long to run this down. If it sounds like he's the one they're after, I can go get him and hold him on suspicion until the warrant clears. Maybe I'll give the newspapers a call, too, and let them in on it. He's probably trying to run and hide like a scared rabbit, but he won't get away with that, either."

Kimberly's eyes ignited with fury as she came to her feet. "Doing your job is one thing, Sheriff, but bringing the press into this before you have any proof is going too far. Jason came to Nevada to be left alone. What you're talking about now is totally unnecessary and cruel. I wouldn't blame him if he—if he—"

"If he what?" demanded Muller.

"Hold on now. Let's everybody just calm down," said Giz evenly. "This thing is bigger than some of our personal problems that keep flaring up around here. The whole country's going to be watching what happens with this story. If we say it's him and it turns out we're wrong, Austin will be the laughing stock of the entire United States. This town's not much, but still, I don't want that happening."

Fred and Digger nodded in agreement as Kimberly glared at the sheriff. "Well, Bob," she said. "What's it going to be?"

"Tell you what I'll do," he began, after a short pause, his voice suspiciously calm. "I won't do anything at all until I'm positive he's the one they're after. But I can hardly be held responsible for the story leaking out. Half the town's heard it by now. You saw everybody running out of here, and you all know how word gets around Austin."

"Got a point there," said Fred, as Muller turned and swaggered over to the window of the restaurant. "It sure won't be a secret for long!"

"It's a tough break," added Giz regretfully. "I know he likes his privacy. But you know—there's something else about this we haven't thought of."

"What?" asked Kimberly.

"Those Arabs. They seem to thrive on revenge-type killing. If they get word that Jason did in five of their own people, it seems to me they might want to get some payback. Show the world you don't mess with their kind. They'll have to save face somehow. They can't let one lone American kill five of their best."

"But if it was him, I mean our Jason," said Digger, "they'd have him in jail or some kind of protective custody by the time them terrorists could get all the way out here."

"Yeah, but they've been known to plant bombs most anywhere and don't care who all they kill. They might even plant one right in the courthouse of his trial or some place like that. They're good at that sort of thing, and they've sure had enough practice at it over the years."

"But other than 9-11, nothing like that has ever happened over here," objected Kimberly.

Giz glanced at Kimberly. "I think they were just about to start when Jason, or whoever, put an end to it. If that's the case, if the terrorists were going to start up in this country, with their bombs and murdering, then they'll almost have to get Jason, just to prove to the world they're to be taken seriously."

Bob Muller smirked, as if Giz's ideas were ridiculous, but then his eyes narrowed in thought.

For a moment, Fred seemed puzzled, then asked slowly, "What if they decide not to arrest this 'Jason'? And let's just say it is our Jason. What happens if the papers and such let it out that it was him and tells where he's at, where he lives?"

As soon as the question ended, a wave of realization hit the small group, except the sheriff, who was already two steps ahead of them.

"We can't let the story get out!" announced Kimberly.

"How can we stop it now?" asked Digger.

"Everybody in town knows Jason," said Kimberly, as a spark of hope showed in her eyes. "And except for Bob, I think everyone likes him. If a story can spread in a small town about one thing, it can certainly spread about another. We can put the word out to everyone that Jason's life is at stake, and they have to keep quiet about what they've heard today."

Shaking his head enthusiastically, Fred said, "We can do it, too! We know everybody that could've or would've heard. We have to do it quick, though, or it'll be too late."

Digger grinned broadly, his wiry body brimming with energy, "Hot damn! Now we're talkin'!"

CHAPTER ELEVEN

McWilliams rose early the next morning, and when Burkhart entered the kitchen, the table was waiting with fried potatoes, toast, sausage, and eggs covered with Tabasco sauce. Taking it all in, Burkhart grunted. "Making you head cook was the smartest thing I've done in quite a while."

Filling their cups with pitch-black coffee, McWilliams took a seat. "Better eat up, or this Joe will strip the wallpaper off your insides."

"Good. Then it will keep my eyes open."

"So what's up for today? I'm game for anything."

"Well, I was up half the night thinking about that. I decided its best that we go about our ranching business like nothing much has happened. But we keep our guns close, and while we work, we'll be thinking about what all could happen and how we could handle it. At night, we'll make whatever plans we come up with. We should have several days, at least, before we have to worry too much about any serious trouble."

Forking potatoes onto his plate, McWilliams said, "Sounds good to me. We behave like nothing unusual is goin' on."

"Today, Mac, I want you to take some of the maps Digger gave us and scout out the rangeland. Calculate the carrying capacity for our cattle, but keep a lookout for anything we might be able to use defensively—if we have need to head out that way."

"What'll you be up to?"

"I've got some rough ideas in my head. I'm going to plant the canteens in parts of the desert that we can find easily if we have to. I'm going by horseback and taking some of the rougher trails—trails that no vehicle can follow. I'll take another trail out towards an old mining area I know about. I figure that if they come at us, they'll come on foot or use some sort of four-wheeler. They won't think of horses."

McWilliams eyed Burkhart appraisingly. "You ever been in the military?"

"No."

"Maybe you shoulda been. You think like a natural-born army man."

Burkhart took a bite of eggs and washed it down with coffee. "Just common sense."

"While I was cooking this morning, I thought of some good that come of yesterday in that café."

"I think you must have been born an optimist, Mac. What possible good came out of that disaster?"

"Kimberly. She at least can figure out why you give her the cold shoulder. It won't take her no time to put it together."

Jason continued eating in silence, but occasionally glanced up at Mac. Finally, he said, "I don't want to sound like the half-empty glass, but I'm not so sure. Maybe she'll just think I've got too much on my mind—that she's not important to me anymore—or maybe she lost interest in me the minute she found out what I did. Who knows anything, anymore?"

McWilliams smiled. "Boss, anybody can see I ain't an educated man, at least in schooling. But the Lord give me two things I come by natural. I know cows, and I know people. I knew what you'd do on that airplane, and I know what Kimberly's going to do, too. She'll stick by you because she knows a real man when she sees one. You can go to the bank on it, Jason. She's a keeper, son, a rare one."

"I hope you're right, Mac," said Jason, "but it still doesn't change anything. I can't see her—I can't be involved in her life. Not for a long, long time."

After both men had cleaned their plates and finished one last cup of coffee, McWilliams took the shotgun and several maps, then drove off to familiarize himself with the range allotments. With fifty thousand acres to cover, it would be near sundown before he returned.

Keeping the maps of the most remote parts of the backcountry for himself, Burkhart watched McWilliams disappear, then began filling the five canteens. When he finished, he loaded them into his saddlebags, along with several packages of beef jerky. Very carefully, he added a small bundle wrapped in plain brown paper. Shoving the entire bundle against the wall of the kitchen, away from the stove, Burkhart unfolded the maps and spread them on the table.

For hours, he examined every square mile, noting the terrain, arroyos, trails, old mines—he even found a promising spring. Stopping occasionally, however, he paused to scan the horizon beyond the window and glance at Trouble, who lay sleeping at his feet.From now on, he would have to be keenly aware of everything around him. He would have to be alert, even to the subtlest changes, and wary of anything that hinted of danger. If he and Mac were to have a chance, they would have to consider themselves under siege and be prepared to defend themselves against any conceivable attack.

Their most effective defense against a terrorist attack lay in their isolation and the inability of anyone to approach during daylight without being seen. At night, without lights to guide them, anyone unfamiliar with the desert would be hard-pressed to find them. Their weakest link would be in securing supplies, and that had Burkhart worried, for Mac, not he, would be the one going to town to get them.

Shortly after sunset, Trouble's ears twitched, and he came to his feet with his head cocked to one side. A moment later, Burkhart heard the rattling of the Willys as it bounded its way over the rough road and came to a dusty stop in front of the house.

"You get lost out there?" jested Burkhart.

"Almost. That country just keeps on a goin'. If I hadn't been tryin' to save on gas, I'd still be runnin' around out there."

"It's a big country. Clean and wide open. That's why I like it here. There's a sense of freedom out there I don't get anywhere else."

Mac stepped onto the porch and removed his sweat-stained hat. "There is that, my friend, but when you're out there, you're on your own. Any help is sure to be a long way off."

"That's all in our favor."

"You get done what you wanted with those canteens?"

Burkhart shook his head. He wore a faint, almost imperceptible smile. "After studying my maps, I decided to wait until tomorrow."

Over a dinner of huevos rancheros and ham, the two men reviewed the ranching operation in more detail, but spent most of the night discussing the lay of the land, defensible rock formations, and locations of connecting arroyos. When they were ready to call it a day, Burkhart paused in the doorway of his bedroom. "By the way Mac, I'll be leaving early tomorrow and won't be back for two days."

"Leavin'! For where?"

"The same place you were today, but I'll leave you the pickup. I'm taking the Appaloosa."

"What'll you do for water?"

"There's a spring I found on my maps. I'll be alright."

Shaking his head, McWilliams yawned, "Anything in particular you want me to do while you're gone?"

"Most everything needs some sort of repair. You're a better judge than I am on what should have priority. But above all, Mac, keep a constant eye on that road out there.

Watch for anything that seems out of place. Trouble will be here to help out, and I think it's best we don't have any light showing after sundown."

"Good idea. I think it's early for us to have any visitors, but we ought to be gettin' in the habit, sure enough. But you be careful your ownself, too."

"My middle name," smiled Burkhart weakly, then vanished into an unlit bedroom.

Fatigued by the long day and a previous restless night's sleep, McWilliams did not awaken to the muffled sounds stirring in the pre-dawn darkness. Nor did he hear Trouble whining plaintively as Burkhart ordered him to stay behind, then return to offer an explanation. "You have to stay, boy," he whispered, scratching the hound affectionately behind the ear. "Water will be hard enough to come by without having to worry about you."

With a final pat on the head, Burkhart hefted the saddlebags he had brought out from the kitchen and headed for the corral. After haltering and saddling the gelding, he tied the saddlebags on securely and checked them for balance.

Behind the cantle, he tied a canvas bedroll and wool blanket. Adding the rifle boot last, he slid in the 30-30, then, after adjusting his Colt to a more comfortable position, swung into the saddle.

The stars were beginning to fade when he rode into the cool air of the desert morning, and except for the creak of leather and clacking of steel clad hooves over rocky ground, all was serenely quiet.

Finding Jason already gone, Travis McWilliams selected his first project while he ate a quick breakfast. Taking his coffee in one hand and his shotgun in the other, he went out the back door and cautiously approached the sagging outhouse. Warily, he circled it, noting several breaks in the old wooden foundation that were as good as engraved invitations to rats and snakes, especially to rattlesnakes.

As he studied the problem and drank his coffee, he heard Trouble barking in the distance. Taking a few steps to his left, McWilliams could see past the corner of the house and more than a mile of the road that led to the ranch. A half-mile out, coming slowly towards him, was a single white pickup truck.

He watched closely as the hound charged the intruder then mysteriously quit barking. The dog turned abruptly and followed along in silence as the truck came steadily closer. Taking one last drink of coffee, McWilliams moved to the front of the house and set the cup on the front porch. He wanted both hands free should he need to operate the pump-action scattergun.

With the morning sun glaring on the dusty windshield, it was difficult to see inside the cab, but as the driver neared, McWilliams began to relax. There was only one person visible, and it was definitely a woman.

"Hello, Travis."

McWilliams recognized the voice before he could make out the face. "Miss Kimberly," he said cheerfully. "I was hoping you would come by."

"You were?" asked Kimberly, eyeing the shotgun.

"Sure I was. How are you this morning?"

Kimberly shrugged. "I've been better. But how are you? You seem to be in a good mood."

"Oh, I'm doin' fine. I was just starting to close down the rattlesnake hotel we got out back."

Glancing at McWilliams, Kimberly asked, "That old outhouse?"

"You guessed it."

Pausing to look around, Kimberly turned off the truck's engine. "Is Jason around? I'd like—no, I need to talk to him about yesterday."

"Sorry. He lit out this morning before daylight. He was gone when I got up. Left on horseback and said he wouldn't be back for two days. And didn't say why or where to."

Obviously disappointed, Kimberly sat inside her truck, her face a testament of uncertainty. "Two days? What could he be doing for two days all alone?

McWilliams sighed, then smiled. "Come on in and have some coffee. You look like you could use some."

"Thanks," said Kimberly, as she stepped out of the truck and gave Trouble a pat on the head. "It's been a long—well what has it been? A day and a half. It seems so much longer with all that's been happening. But I do have some good news."

McWilliams opened the screen door for Kimberly and led her to the kitchen table. "We can use all the good news we can get," he said, then filled a heavy porcelain mug and slid it across the table. "Have a seat."

Taking the cup with both hands, she took a sip. "Giz, Matty, Digger, and I got in touch with everyone—I mean everyone. The response was sort of like after we all heard about the Twin Towers. People started putting out their flags. The whole town came together, and we're certain no one will talk to the media or anyone else. The fact that Jason is here won't get out. His secret is safe.

"I'm so proud of us—our little community. I've never seen it like this. We're protecting one of our own; everyone will be looking out for the two of you."

McWilliams beamed. "Just like small town folks. I wish Jason could have heard that before he left, especially from you. He could use some cheering up about now."

Kimberly took another drink of coffee and gazed out the window into the desert. "How is he Travis? I mean really. How is he?"

"Hard to say, Kimberly. He's full of fight, but he feels boxed in, like there's no way to win. He don't see any way out, but to stay here and make a stand. He ain't of a mind to run. But as far as it all goes, I don't think he's lookin' too awful far down the road. He has his hands full with just the here and now."

There was moment of silence before Kimberly spoke again. "Did Jason," she began timidly, "say anything—about me? I mean, since yesterday?"

McWilliams looked at Kimberly Whitney. Her eyes reflected a beautiful sadness, an exquisite blend of anxiety and compassion that only a young woman in love could embrace. "Ms. Kimberly," he said admiringly, "that's why I'm glad you stopped by. I think it's important you know a little more than you do. He don't believe it hisself, but he needs you to know. Now, maybe I shouldn't say this, but I'm goin' to, for both your sakes. And I hope you'll understand. He wants you to stay away from him—more than he wants to be near you."

Kimberly blinked. "Then he truly doesn't want to see me anymore?"

"Oh, no," said McWilliams, waving a hand. "Let me chew that a little bit finer. There's only one thing he wants more than to see you again—and that is to keep you safe. You see, he's givin' you up, givin' up what he dearly wants—for you."

Shaking her head, Kimberly said anxiously, "But I'm in no danger. Why should he be trying to protect me?"

"He believes they might try and kill you if them terrorists think you mean something to him. And Jason's not alone in that regard. There's at least one high-up FBI agent that agrees with him. If word does get out it was him that did that shooting, he's likely to be a marked man, not by our law, but by them damned terrorists. Anybody close to him will be a target, too.

"They'll likely come out here looking for him as soon as they find out where he's at. Probably one of them sleeper cells we keep hearing about. Anyways, it's a chance Jason ain't willing to take, not with the woman he loves."

Shock displaced Kimberly's disbelief; slowly, as McWilliams' words began to register, she started to smile, as tears welled up in her eyes. "Then you tell him," she said, taking McWilliams' hand and squeezing it. "When he gets back, you tell that Jason Burkhart that I'll keep my distance if that's what he wants. But I won't be scared off, and I won't let him give me up!"

McWilliams patted her hand. "That a-girl. That's the kind of woman a man needs. You'll do, Ms. Kimberly; you'll do just fine!"

CHAPTER TWELVE

The first day of Burkhart's absence was totally occupied with Kimberly's visit and the reconstruction of the outhouse foundation. But on the morning of the second day, McWilliams sat alone at breakfast, analyzing why Jason Burkhart had gone off by himself, where he had gone, and how far on horseback. However, considering the fact that he had offered only a vague explanation, Mac understood the matter to be private. Yet still, he wondered. Did he need time alone, time to work through his feelings for Kimberly, or just simply a chance to recuperate from the stress of the last few days? Or perhaps, just perhaps, there was an entirely different reason.

McWilliams smiled as he thought of the most likely answer. Could he already have a plan to work out? Had he developed something that would risk but one man, a plan that could be orchestrated by only one man—one man alone, in the harsh isolation of the unending Nevada desert?

Suddenly convinced that he had guessed correctly, and feeling more at ease, McWilliams gave the matter no more thought and spent the rest of the morning working in the barn, repairing tack. Keeping a watchful eye on the road that led into the ranch and casting a periodic glance in the direction of the Appaloosa's day-old tracks, he worked steadily until the sun was high overhead. It was nearing one o'clock when he pulled out his pocket watch and decided to break for lunch, but as he neared the house, he pulled up suddenly.

From the shady side of the house, he heard Trouble snarl, then saw him come to his feet and stare into the distance. Looking in the same direction as the hound, McWilliams caught a distant flash of light, followed closely by another. Someone was coming in on the road, and from the looks of the dust rising, they were driving fast.

Running to his bedroom, McWilliams slammed a shell into the chamber of the pump shotgun, then filled his pockets with extra shells. Moving quickly to the front room, he knelt down beside the window as the hairs on the dog's neck bristled. Trouble began barking wildly.

When the intruders crested a ridge, still a mile from the house, Mac swallowed hard and swore. Coming at a high rate of speed was not one vehicle but a string of at least a dozen! As they closed in, he swore more bitterly. Walking onto the porch, he leaned the shotgun against the wall. At the head of the line was the familiar white patrol car of the county sheriff.

In a cloud of dust, with a battery of slamming doors, a small army of zealots emerged from the caravan with bazooka-like armaments slung over their shoulders. "This is it," bellowed the sheriff haughtily, "be it ever so humble."

"What do you want, and what in hell are all these people doin' here?" demanded McWilliams.

"I decided to invite some of your friends out," said the sheriff, waving a hand at the crowd, then added sarcastically, "Don't you recognize the 'people's right to know' when you see it, old man? They want your boss on all the TV stations so everybody can see him. I think your game of hide and seek is over."

"You got any papers?" asked McWilliams, eyeing the reporters with disgust.

"Not yet," admitted Muller arrogantly, "but they'll come."

"All right then, you, and everybody else, get off this land," ordered McWilliams. "You're trespassing. Do you hear? Get off this ranch!"

In unison, the mob protested angrily. McWilliams waved his hand to quiet them, just as another pickup drove up and skidded to a stop. "Sheriff, you got no right to be here if you're not doin' business, and for certain, none of them newshounds has any right to come here, either. You know as well as I do that Burkhart's goin' to be a target for those murderin' terrorists. If you people shoot your mouths off all over the country and show where he lives, he's as good as dead."

"Who's the murderer here?" yelled a voice from the crowd. "Let's hear him defend himself. What about the pilot?"

"He didn't even give them a chance," said another, as others chimed in agreeably.

"So that's how it is," growled McWilliams contemptuously, then turned for the shotgun.

Lunging forward, Muller grabbed McWilliams by the shirt collar and with a viscous jerk backwards, nearly lifted him from the floor of the porch. Then, forcing his arms behind his back, the sheriff demanded, "Now, where is he?"

"He's not here, and hasn't been for two days," answered McWilliams, gritting against the pain. "I guess he didn't listen to your orders, did he?"

"You lied to us, Bob!" exclaimed an angry voice, as a young woman shoved her way through the crowd. "You didn't wait!"

"Kimberly!" exclaimed Muller, as a hush covered the curious onlookers.

"Mac said he's not here! Now let him go," demanded Kimberly, unaware of the many news cameras now focused on her.

"Well, now!" rang out another voice, a voice that by its very tone commanded attention. "Mac's been known to be wrong now and then."

Robotically, the cameras swung around as all eyes shifted to the speaker behind them. Sitting astride an

Appaloosa, unshaven, covered in trail dust, was a powerfully built man whose expression was shaded by the flat-brimmed hat he wore. In one hand, he held split leather reins, and in his other, a long-barreled Colt .45. And there was no question where the sights were aimed.

Burkhart nudged the gelding into the crowd, and the sea of cameras divided. "You heard the lady, Sheriff," he said calmly.

Staring into the ominous black hole of the Colt, Muller relaxed his hold on McWilliams and stepped back. Mac limbered his arms and shoulder, then smiled broadly. "You got back early, Boss."

"You all right?" asked Burkhart, his eyes riveted on Muller.

"Yep."

"I take it those cameras are running?"

"Seems so."

"Your shotgun loaded?"

Mac chuckled. "Yep," he said as he picked it up and laid it into the fold of his arm.

"You ever shoot clay pigeons, Mac?"

Mac nodded, his eyes narrowing, "Once or twice."

With his pistol carefully trained on the sheriff, Burkhart dismounted, and with a slap on the rump, sent the horse to the barn. "Then you won't have any trouble with those 'vultures' they're carrying. So have at it."

As Burkhart stepped up onto the porch, Mac's face was blank, but then in a flash of illumination, he understood, and started lining everyone in a single file. Ordering them at gunpoint to stand still, he took a few steps back.

Kimberly's eyes opened wide. "Jason, what are you doing?"

Ignoring her question, he said, "When you're ready, Mac."

McWilliams nodded and yelled, "PULL!"

First in line was a hawk-nosed, narrow-shouldered man who looked at McWilliams stupidly.

"Throw it up!" demanded McWilliams impatiently. "The camera, damn it! Throw it up now, or I'll shoot it out of your hands!"

"But this is company property," howled the cameraman bitterly. "Who do you—"

McWilliams laid the barrel of the 12-gauge behind the objector's left ear and cocked the hammer back. A split second later, the 'vulture' flew high and was immediately and expertly blasted from existence.

As if sewn together, the entire line flinched from the concussion. Several high-pitched screams erupted, some of them from women, some of them from men.

"You," ordered Mac, pointing at the first thrower, "End of the line. And let's have the next one up here."

Five minutes later, the job was done. Only fragments of black plastic and glimmering glass lay scattered on the sand. "Almost out of shells," commented McWilliams, as he stepped into the shade to reload from his pockets.

"I think we made our point," said Burkhart, still staring at Muller. "At least with the press."

"You're insane," screeched a near hysterical female. "You can't get away with this. What about the freedom of the press? Do you think you're more important than that? We have a right—the people have a right—you'll pay for this!"

McWilliams glared hatefully at the reporters, who stared back with eyes full of anger and fear. "No freedom is absolute. But I suppose you folks think yourselves above it all. No need for a conscience, no use for common sense at all!"

"There's nothing common about sense, Mac," said Burkhart. "It's ignorance that's all too common."

"Guess you're right, Jason," replied McWilliams, then reached his hand into an empty pocket. "I need another box of buckshot."

Gasping in disbelief, the line of reporters collapsed into a horrified cluster, watching McWilliams enter the house and return with another box of ammunition. “What now?” he asked.

Burkhart unbuckled his gun belt with his left hand and handed it to Kimberly, then he handed her his hat. “Take off your belt and pistol, Muller,” he ordered. “And your backup pistol, too.”

Suddenly, McWilliams seemed unsure. “You sure you want to do this, Boss?”

As Muller dropped his belted gun and removed his ankle pistol, Kimberly asked nervously, “What are you doing, Jason? You can’t expect to fight him. You can’t win. You don’t know what he’s capable of. Jason, he’ll hurt you!”

“Well, well,” muttered Muller, breaking into a confident smile. “Kimberly’s afraid for your health. Now that’s real touching.” Then, conceitedly, he added as he stepped down off the porch and out into the sun, “I’m going to do to you what I should have done months ago.”

Sizing up the opponent, Mac whispered warningly to Jason, “He’s big and strong. Keep your distance, and wear him down. Use the heat against him. You’ll have to outlast him before you can finish him.”

Handing over the Colt, Burkhart nodded, then left the porch. Recognizing what was occurring, assured of the outcome, the excited crowd hungrily encircled the two antagonists. With vicarious bravery, and blood in their eyes, they jeered vengefully, lusting for Burkhart’s destruction.

Spreading both arms wide, Muller grinned mockingly, “This spot okay?”

“Your choice,” replied Burkhart coldly as he worked the stiffness from his left arm.

With three inches in height and forty pounds to his advantage, Muller stood smugly, relishing the moment. He would annihilate Burkhart in front of an audience, and in front of Kimberly. Perhaps he would even kill him with his bare fists.

His hands resting easily on his hips, Muller started pompously, "I'm going to—"

Without warning, Burkhart moved in with a lightning-fast jab, chopping off Muller's next word and splitting both lips. The big head barely moved from the impact, but instantly, Muller's arms coiled, and with surprising agility, he took a quick step to the left.

Burkhart feinted with his right and caught the corner of a rib with a powerful left hook. Muller grunted, but countered with a smashing right to the jaw that staggered Burkhart and rang his ears.

Pausing to gloat, Muller glanced at Kimberly, but the expression on her face only enraged him, and he lunged for Burkhart, reaching for his throat.

Instinctively, Burkhart dropped to his knees, and the hulking sheriff stumbled over him, plowing into the hard packed sand and gravel. Yet as suddenly as he landed, he was on his feet, but Burkhart, already waiting, landed a right uppercut squarely on the chin. This time, the head snapped back as Muller was rocked on his heels by the shockingly powerful blow.

Again Burkhart moved in, but Muller deflected a left-right combination and managed to recover his balance. Then, furiously swinging with both fists, he knocked Burkhart to the ground and viciously tried to stomp his head, missing by inches. Burkhart rolled twice, missing another kick, and scrambled to his feet, fully aware of what Muller had attempted to do.

With momentum on his side, Muller came in close. Now anxious to end the fight, he set his feet solidly and threw a deadly right cross. Before it could land, Burkhart slammed a boot heel into Muller's kneecap, tearing it out of place. Muller's leg buckled and his cross went wild, as

Burkhart buried a pointed elbow into the exposed rib cage, then swung around behind to grab a head full of hair. With his left hand, he ripped Muller's head backwards and savagely rammed a half-fist into the exposed Adams apple.

Tottering on one leg, Muller bent over, choking badly, grasping his throat with both hands. A crushing blow to the kidney straightened him up long enough to offer a shot to his unprotected diaphragm that folded him again, but this time left him unable to breath. Then with a sledgehammer blow to the temple, Burkhart dropped the crumpled sheriff into the dust.

Landing flat on his face, he slowly rolled over on his back. A moment later, he began to breath. But that was all.

Burkhart caught his breath, then shoved his way past the shocked spectators as Kimberly and McWilliams, awe-struck, looked on. Taking the shotgun from inside the sheriff's truck, he smashed it against a large rock. Throwing the pieces on the seat, he turned and pointed to two bystanders. "You and you, load him up and drive him out of here."

As the two men struggled to get the sheriff loaded, Burkhart paused to study the faces before him. Seeing the indignation and feeling their self-righteous judgment bearing down on him, he said, in a clear commanding voice, "I killed to prevent murder. I killed in self-defense. But in the name of journalism, some, if not all of you, are going to be accomplices to my murder. When you hear of my death, you'll arrogantly shrug and regurgitate 'the people's right to know' on every station and in every form of print imaginable. But God help this country if it lets the media use the Constitution of the United States as a license to kill innocent people!"

Walking past Kimberly, he took the belt and holster from her, and from McWilliams, he took the Colt. Then, in a bone-chilling tone, he demanded, "Now get off my land!"

Keeping his eyes on the retreating reporters and without turning his head, Burkhart added softly, "You shouldn't have come, Kimberly. Leave with them. Don't answer any questions that might link us. I don't want you involved in this."

Kimberly glanced at Jason's bruised face, a face she desperately wanted to kiss, but instead, she turned to McWilliams and flashed a courageous smile. "Why should I be involved," she said seriously. "After all, you are just a neighbor of mine, someone I just met a few days ago. There won't be a problem."

When the reporters were out of hearing distance, she reluctantly started for her pickup, but stopped suddenly and spun around. "The old-timers around here have a saying: 'It ain't over 'til the fat lady sings,' and I say she's nowhere in sight. There's always hope, and I don't see you as a quitter. I'm to stay away from you Jason Burkhart, but I'm not going away!"

Burkhart looked questioningly at McWilliams as Kimberly walked back to her truck. "What was that all about?"

Mac smoothed his mustache with the back of his knuckles to hide his smile. "She's a dandy, Jason. She's a dandy."

Lowering his pistol and holstering it, Burkhart mumbled bitterly, "Too soon, or maybe too late. I don't know which."

"What's that?"

"Women like her make living easy, but they make dying a hell of a lot harder. I'm glad she's out of it."

"Yep. It's sure enough goin' to hit the fan now, but at least we started the ball with style. We sent 'em home with their tails tucked today."

"Yeah, Mac, but they're going to scream like scalded dogs."

CHAPTER THIRTEEN

The week passed slowly, with both men half-heartedly keeping busy with daily chores, but not accomplishing anything of consequence. Why there hadn't been repercussions from the reporters or the law, neither could guess, but wherever the two of them went, they were armed. As the days passed, however, their expectations turned into a growing anxiety, and even with Trouble tied outside the house at night, sleep was sporadic at best.

Long before the first light of Saturday morning, Burkhart opened his eyes and stared into the darkness. Doubting he had slept at all, he threw off his blanket and sat up on the edge of the bed. Two fluorescent lines told him it was only four-thirty, but he lit a kerosene lantern to dress, and after turning down the wick, went into the kitchen. Setting the dim light on the floor, he filled the coffee pot with water and lit the stove.

"Might as well make enough for two," said a muffled voice from the second bedroom. "I couldn't sleep, neither."

"Glad to have the company," replied Burkhart, as Mac shuffled into the kitchen with his eyes half open and a shotgun in his elbow.

The water came to a boil, and Burkhart flipped the lid and dropped in a handful of grounds. "I forgot to mention it the other day," he began as he took the pot from the flame, "but when I was riding the range earlier, I came across one of the Whitney bulls. It had wandered way off. Thought I'd ride out and get it today and either drive it back, or bring it in."

Mac held out his cup, and nodded. "Kind of thought I'd go to town today. Pick up our supplies if they're in." A coyote yipped eerily into the night, its cry carried through the open window on a breath of cool wind. After the sound faded, McWilliams began again. "And we need to know what's happened lately. Somethin's just not right. Somethin' shoulda happened after what we did."

Smiling weakly over his coffee, Burkhart agreed, "You would think they'd have sent the troopers in after us." Taking a sip of coffee, he continued more somberly, "But you're right. Something should have happened by now. I can only guess that the warrant still hasn't been finalized. And as for Muller—who knows."

"That sure don't figure," mumbled McWilliams. "And after that whippin' you gave him, to boot."

"Be sure to stay away from him when you go in, Mac. No telling what he might try to do."

"I'll dang sure do my best, but I don't think he's interested too much in me. Do you think the news folks kept quiet? There might be a paper, to see if they did."

Burkhart grunted cynically. "They did what they could. Without pictures, their story wasn't as glamorous, but I'm sure they broadcast everything they could think of, and then some, just to spice it up. News is a product these days. If it's not splashy, flashy, or bloody, it doesn't sell. The only question now is how long we have before the terrorists try to even the score."

"Well, at least on that," said McWilliams optimistically, "we ought to get some help from the Feds. They won't let just anybody into this country. They kinda know who those people are don't they? Or the CIA, maybe?"

"Yeah, Mac. But what if they're here already? Maybe they were here before, or maybe they've been here for years. In California, there are thousands of immigrants from that part of the world. And they've all arrived recently, too. It's hard to believe some extremists haven't filtered in with the good ones."

By the time breakfast had been cooked and eaten, only the morning star remained on the eastern horizon, but the rest of the sky was still dark and glimmering. As the dawn grew brighter, however, Burkhart's mood grew foreboding. Uneasily, he went to his room and checked his saddlebags, making sure the extra shells were there, even though he knew they were. As if answering to a sixth sense, he added the small brown packet, then buckled the flaps down tight. Throwing the bags over his shoulder and grabbing his pistol belt and rifle, he returned to the kitchen where Mac sat waiting. "Wait until I'm over the hill, Mac, then let Trouble off the chain and give him a big bowl of food. He'll stay put when you drive away."

Pausing to strap on his Colt, he glanced up anxiously. "And Mac," he added softly, "take your shotgun with you today. There's something—"

"I know, Jason," interrupted McWilliams. "I feel it too. Likely, it's just nerves. But I learned a long time ago to trust my gut feelin's. Don't worry, I'll go armed."

Burkhart started to leave, but hesitated. "Travis," he began awkwardly, "I want you to know—Well, I can't tell you how much I appreciate you being here and standing by me in all of this."

Travis McWilliams stood and extended his arm. Solemnly, they shook hands, their eyes revealing an understanding that needed no explanation.

"Vaya con dios, Jason. Until we meet again, my friend."

With lips drawn tight, Burkhart lifted his hat from the wall and nodded. "Until then," he said clearly, then stepped past McWilliams and out the front door. Stopping beside Trouble, he knelt and scratched him affectionately, then pulled him close and gave him a hug. Glancing at the fading sky, he muttered, "The 'fat lady' sings today."

CHAPTER FOURTEEN

Only the brightest stars lingered in the gray-blue sky when Burkhart started working his way over the hills. As the last one faded, he turned the gelding onto the old Pony Express trail. Continuing in a westerly direction, he began to climb steadily, until he reached the pass just south of Eagle Butte and dropped out of reach of the rising sun and into the shadows of the steep western slope. Now in Piñon pine and cedar, he followed the Express trail another two miles before reaching the open desert. An hour later, he cut the trail of the bull, finally coming on him in Rye Patch Canyon.

Pure black, and weighing a good ton and a half, the Angus-Brahma cross had been bred for aggressiveness on the range, and it was close to noon before the dust settled and the bull was on the old trail headed for the ranch. But for a precious few hours, Burkhart had thought of nothing save the bull, his horse, and the desert terrain.

As the hulking breed plodded slowly in front of him, Burkhart gradually relaxed into his saddle, feeling nothing but the sun's warmth on his shoulders, and hearing only the sound of leather and hooves. Twisting to gaze over his shoulder, his eyes swept across endless miles of unspoiled land that stretched quietly under a clean blue sky, and for a sheltering moment, he was at peace. Here was where he wanted to be, doing what he had grown to love, asking nothing of anyone but to be left alone. For the first time in a seemingly endless week, his mind was at ease, his thoughts were more ordered, and his perspective strangely altered.

Turning back around, however, he saw the Butte rising ominously in front of him, and beneath it, the passage he must take. On the other side, he knew the futile, desperate world from which he had come lay waiting for his return. As he stared morosely at the barrier, a wave of buried emotion slammed into him. Jolted by the gut-wrenching surge of adrenaline, Burkhart instinctively jerked on the split reins, bringing the startled gelding to an abrupt halt. Swearing bitterly, he thought of what was ahead of him, but when he had recovered from the sobering reverberations of reality, Jason Burkhart realized something had changed. He had changed!

The despair, the acceptance, the hopelessness was gone. In its place lurked something angry, primordial, and something fiercely defensive.

Impulsively spurring the Appaloosa to a trot, he pushed the bull up and over the pass. Pausing on the summit to rest the animals, Burkhart slid his rifle out of the scabbard and brushed off a few bits of cedar that had fallen in, then opened the action slightly to make sure it was clean. After replacing the rifle, he double-checked the leather ties holding his saddlebags and retied one, making it more secure.

Easing up on the reins, Burkhart let the gelding have his head, knowing he would retrace his tracks back to the ranch. After beginning the descent, the bull, too, seemed to know the way, and for the most part, stayed on the narrow wagon road with little encouragement. The further down the eastern slope they went, however, the more alert Burkhart became, his senses sharpening with each step. When he turned off the Express trail and crested a small knoll above the ranch house, he was as wary as any cougar and as poised.

"Easy, Apache," he said softly, as he reined in and patted the horse's neck. Looking down the gentle grade to the house, he could see Trouble lying in the shade of the porch, apparently asleep. Nothing else caught his attention, except the missing pickup. “You should be back by now, Mac,” he mumbled to himself. As the gelding turned its ears back, waiting for instructions, Burkhart eased up on the leathers, and the horse started forward, keeping one ear to the rear, while pointing the other expectantly to the trail ahead.

Cautiously, meticulously, Burkhart squinted against the glare, sweeping the area surrounding the house and corrals, looking for anything that might be out of place. Twice, he stopped and listened for ten minutes before proceeding. Finally, he reached the outer gate, some three hundred yards out, and dismounted to open it.

Remounting, he pushed the bull through the gate, then watched as it wandered towards the grass that grew in back of the corrals. All seemed well enough, until a small cloud of dust took shape in the distance. Someone was on the road, coming in slowly.

Logic told him it was McWilliams returning, but with the hairs on the back of his neck raising up, Burkhart grabbed the rifle and laid it on his lap. With the barn and a good bucket of oats waiting ahead, Apache sharply jerked at the bit but was held back firmly. This was no time to make assumptions, to behave predictably. It was time, however, to trust what Mac had called his ‘gut feelin’, to play the hunch, or simply and perhaps, more accurately, rely on pure instinct.

Dismounting once more to close the gate and latch it, he kept the rifle in hand and stood in the narrow shadow cast by the heavy cedar gatepost. Trouble was now coming to his feet. Shortly, the familiar wailing began as he called out his greeting to the approaching truck.

“What do you know,” shrugged Burkhart, “it is Mac, after all.”

Leaning against the weathered post, he relaxed for a moment, and watched the dog as it began trotting up the dusty road towards the Willys just coming into sight. As the dog approached the oncoming pickup, Burkhart started to turn, but suddenly, the hound veered away from the road and came to a halt. Instead of following the truck as usual, Trouble raised his nose high in the air. A second later, the high-pitched bark of warning reached Burkhart's ears. Raising the rifle and resting it on a cross post with one hand, he wrapped the reins tightly around it with his other. "What did you smell, Trouble?" he asked, then levered a shell into the chamber of the Winchester. "And where's Mac?"

Fifty feet from the house, the Willys stopped, and from nowhere, four armed men jumped from the bed of the truck, followed by the driver. With the precision of practiced execution, two went through the front door, and two circled each side of the house, working their way to the rear. The driver remained in front, holding an automatic weapon and shouting orders—not in English or Spanish, but in a tongue all too familiar, the language of terrorists.

Burkhart confidently raised the 30-30's rear sight three notches, then took a bead on the front guard. At first, he aimed at the middle of the chest, but thinking better of it, moved slightly to the left shoulder. "Alright!" he snarled, "you bought your tickets. Now listen to the fat lady sing." Then gently, he squeezed the trigger.

The steel butt-plate kicked hard into the muscle of his shoulder as the muzzle exploded the fragile silence. Apache flinched sharply at the blast of the rifle, but the distant target staggered backwards. Slamming into a porch post, and then falling to his knees, he scrambled back to the truck.

Methodically, Burkhart levered another round into the chamber, but eased the hammer down. The two men on the near side of the house had thrown themselves to the ground and were undoubtedly searching the hillside for movement. The other two had vanished.

Knowing that standing behind the cedar gate would make him difficult to spot, Burkhart swung into the saddle.

Tightening the reins with his left hand and clamping his legs around the barrel of the horse, he cocked the hammer back and fired a second time. The passenger side of the windshield shattered. Immediately, he saw sand kicking its way up the ridge towards him, as the dull rattle of automatic weapons echoed an instant behind. Burkhart hesitated long enough to see all five weapons firing at him, but just before they found the range, he spurred the gelding into a dead run to the top of the knoll. Skidding to a stop at its crest, he turned in a cloud of dust, and recklessly fired again before continuing his escape. But this time, he rode at an easy gallop.

At the bottom of a shallow arroyo, he slowed to a walk, until he was certain he heard the engine of the Willys behind him, then he hurried on to skyline himself on the way to the Pony Express trail. Glancing over his shoulder, the sight of his pursuers sent a grim smile over his dry lips. Once they made it to the old road, he was certain they would be able to make better speed. They might even overtake him, but it was a chance he would have to take, at least for a few miles. After they saw him sticking to the trail, he could take a few short cuts to stay ahead, but he wanted them on the road.

Knowing the Appaloosa was a quick starter, but lacked endurance, Burkhart kept him at a steady run until he reached the pass. Taking a moment to rest before descending through the cedar and pine, he clearly heard the engine and got an occasional glimpse of the truck as it ground its way up the switchbacks towards him. He could see four men in the bed of the truck, but one was lying flat on his back. When they reached the last of the grade, and he was certain he had been spotted, Burkhart charged the gelding down the western side of Eagle Butte, just as the Express riders had done over a century before. But now, instead of a band of Piutes on his tail, he was hunted by mid-eastern terrorists.

A minute later, he heard shots fired. A quick look behind told him he was in danger, and he realized they were closing faster than expected. He could no longer afford to save the gelding and reluctantly spurred him into a full speed run.

Gaining slightly by cutting through the arroyos, he managed to deny them a clear shot, but up ahead was the flat desert terrain, and for a distance, the road would be straight. If he could only make it to the cut-off, he would have the advantage. How much bottom did the Appaloosa possess?

Rounding the last bend, Burkhart leaned forward, his eyes watering from racing through the dry hot air. Through the thundering hooves, he yelled encouragingly, "Come on 'Patch, come on boy!" And for a few precious moments, the gelding gave a little more.

Scarcely one hundred yards into the straight-away, weapons fire again erupted behind him. They were too close and closing rapidly!

Drawing his pistol, Burkhart twisted in the saddle and desperately thumbed off all five rounds. The truck swerved badly nearly ramming a small bolder but quickly recovered. Yet despite the garbled screams from those standing behind the cab, the driver had slowed noticeably.

Reloading on the run, Burkhart holstered the Colt and immediately saw his landmark in front of him. Just as he turned north off the road, the horse stumbled then regained his feet, with more shots echoing off the hill and into the open range; a range that now sent rippling heat waves dancing in the distance as the blazing sun parched the sands and burned the air.

Following his tracks from a few days earlier, Burkhart headed for a small mound of rocks two miles ahead. The change of terrain had slowed the Willys considerably, but it was still coming fast as it bounced its way over rocks and scratched through clumps of juniper and sage. Now confident of his lead, Burkhart rode the last mile to the outcropping at a canter and dismounted.

Removing a piece of sage from in front of a boulder, he took out two cached canteens then walked to the edge of the formation. Unscrewing the black plastic cap from one, he took a long drink and wiped his forehead to clear the sweat from his eyes.

Distorted by hundred degree heat, he could see the truck stuck in the sand and knew it would be a while before they could figure out the gear combination and change to four wheel drive. Crouching in the meager shade offered by the rocks, Burkhart slowly finished his water.

It was the first chance he had had to think of McWilliams and what happened to him, but with the terrorists in possession of the Willys, only one conclusion was possible. Grimly, Burkhart swore then tossed the empty canteen out into plain sight. Keeping a watchful eye on the pickup, he emptied the second canteen into his hat and let the gelding drink it down.

As he tossed the second canteen, a flash of crimson caught his eye, then a second spot and third. On the sand in front of him was a blood trail and it led to the horse!

Burkhart quickly checked over the animal, then swore bitterly when he found blood streaming from a small black hole just to the rear of the saddle blanket on the right flank and a second, lower in the belly. How much damage the bullets had done he could only guess, but he was certain of what had to be done next. And if he were to live, it would have to be done immediately.

Keeping to the lowest ground available and moving through the thickest patches of juniper, Burkhart came to within two hundred yards of the stuck pickup before taking a prone position in a small clearing.

Trying not to alert them, he slowly removed his hat and laid it an arms length in front of him. Then using the hat's crown as a rest, he laid the forestock of the

Winchester snugly into the felt. After adjusting the rear sight and with no need to allow for windage, Burkhart took careful aim at the truck radiator.

Knowing he could not afford to miss and there would be only one chance, he took a deep breath, then let it out slowly.

The one hundred and eighty grain bullet shattered the silence, then a full five seconds later was followed by a second carefully aimed shot at the same target. Burkhart levered in a third but froze suddenly as he heard the grinding of forced gears and the whine of the engine. They had shifted into four-wheel drive!

Scrambling on his stomach across the sand, he reached the brush then bending low, ran full speed back to outcropping. After shoving the rifle in its boot, Burkhart swung into the saddle and cringed as the geldings legs began to quiver under his weight.

"Sorry, 'Patch," he said remorsefully, "but I need all you've got left."

Nudging him gently with his knees, Burkhart urged the gelding into a fast walk. Still moving to the north and momentarily protected by the thick stands of sage and juniper, he was sure he had not been spotted but had no doubts his pursuers were coming in his general direction. A half mile later, he caught a glimpse of the pickup and judging from its speed and direction, realized they had found his trail again.

Taking a chance, he brought the appaloosa to a canter. After a few yards it stumbled badly yet somehow kept its feet and continued on, but the truck was still bearing down with no sign of overheating. Five minutes more and the horse began to falter severely.

Straining his eyes to see the distant landscape, Burkhart began searching for a clump of dead junipers on the top of a lava covered knoll but knew it was too soon. He would never make it on horseback.

Glancing over his shoulder he was shocked to see the pickup less than a quarter mile behind and throwing up dust clouds in high gear! They were coming towards him faster than he would have believed possible.

Instinctively, he spurred the gelding and it jumped at the command, but then crumbled helplessly into the sand, throwing Burkhart as it went down.

Rolling on his shoulder as he hit, Burkhart staggered to his feet and pulled his rifle and saddle bags from the dying horse and kept running.

He had covered no more than three hundred yards before he dropped to his knees on a small rise gasping desperately for air. Then like a badger crazed by the heat, he tore into the sun baked desert floor. Frantically stabbing with his pocketknife and shoveling with his rifle butt, he burrowed for his life. Building a shallow foxhole was now his only hope for survival.

With a few inches of sand and rock piled around him he quickly looked up expecting the worst but saw nothing. Then wiping the gritty sweat from his eyes, he took a second look and saw the stalled truck partially concealed by brush with a cloud of steam rising from its hood. The door he could see, was swung wide open but no one was in sight.

With perhaps one hundred yards between himself and the pickup, Burkhart took a quick but careful look around. Lying as flat as he could, he scanned his perimeter, but continued to pile sand as he turned. The cover surrounding his position was sparse and what there was stood only knee-high at best. And, luckily, he had taken the only high ground within range of their weapons.

After reloading the rifle to its seven round capacity, Burkhart removed a single .45 cartridge from his belt and dropped it into the only empty chamber of his six-shooter and holstered it. Then on second thought he brought it back out and spun the cylinder to clear it of any sand that might cause it to jam.

In a close fire-fight, he knew he wouldn't have a chance, but if he could hold them at a distance until dark, he could at least attempt an escape. He had no intention of making his stand here if it could be avoided. He must draw them still further into the desert, into his country.

Holding the rifle at the ready, he continued to dig and widen the hole using his left hand. If they came at him from all directions he would need room to maneuver quickly, yet most of all he needed time. But it was still hours before sundown and there were at least four of them out there, waiting for the right moment.

Continually searching everything in sight and memorizing what he could, he gradually sank deeper into the foxhole as the wall around him grew steadily higher.

For an hour nothing moved, but then, from the corner of his eye, he detected a flicker of sunlight.

Staying low with his head barely visible, Burkhart turned towards the flash and dug a narrow notch in the sandy berm, then eased his Winchester into place. The cover from where the movement had come was sparse and hard to believe it could conceal a man, yet he was certain of what he had seen. Or was he? Could the heat already be getting to him or his nerves beginning to fray? He wondered as his skin began to crawl.

Suddenly, however, as if painted by an unseen hand, a leg appeared. A leg that had been there all along but only now stood out from the broken shadows of the scrubby plants surrounding it.

The sun's glare blurred the rear sight of the rifle, but the brush guard over the front post shaded it nicely. Wiping a stinging drop of sweat from his right eye, Burkhart took aim. Again, the Winchester's roar broke the deadly quiet and was followed immediately by the dull unmistakable thud of a slug hitting its mark. A split second later, a surprised scream echoed from the rustling branches.

"Now don't go and die on me," sneered Burkhart as he levered in an other round, "not just yet anyway!"

The shadows grew longer and the heat less intense as the hours dragged by, but the remainder of the afternoon was quiet. When the lower rim of the sun crossed the horizon however, Burkhart reached for his saddlebags and removed the long brown package. Unrolling it, he took out one stick of dynamite.

Studying the explosive carefully he mumbled, "Five seconds, no more."

Then using his rifle butt as a cutting board he chopped off all but two inches of the fuse. Shoving the rear end of the stick into the bank of sand he took out a small book of matches and laid them along side.

In a matter of minutes, the shadows melded into the soft light of dusk and with the sky's brightness fading rapidly, Burkhart knew it would be soon. They could not wait for total darkness or he might slip away unseen, but with no need for precision shooting, they would wait until the last light of day. Then it would be too dark for him to see rifle sights but light enough for them to make out a lone figure at the top of a hill. They would charge in full force, spraying bullets as they came!

All that remained to do, all that he could do, was see from which direction they would come and then light the fuse. With luck, the terrorists would avoid a crossfire and not advance from opposite sides. But that, admittedly, was an uncertainty. His life would depend on what strategy they chose…and on the timing of the dynamite fuse.

He should not have overlooked something so obvious, but until he felt the air stirring, he had totally forgotten about the wind! Starting just after sundown as a light breeze it would suddenly increase and blow steadily for several minutes before calming in the coolness of evening. As the first gust brushed by his cheek, he jerked off his hat and swore. Straining his eyes into the twilight, he saw three figures rise from a dark blanket of sage ninety yards to his right. With forty paces between them they moved slowly forward, hunched at the shoulders.

"Come on!" whispered Burkhart frantically as the wind lifted a few grains of sand in front of him, then on impulse he fired a shot in their direction.

Rapid fire burst from all three weapons as each man shouted wildly and broke into a run. Huddled flat on his knees and using the hat to block the swirling wind, Burkhart struck a match. Immediately it blew out!

Fumbling desperately, he ripped another from the pack and shifted his body, bending even lower and moving the fuse deeper into the hat's crown. A barrage of lead riddled the make-shift barricade, covering him with sand. Amid the thunderous rattle of gunfire, he struck the second match and held it on the fuse a half-inch from its base. With a bursting flash, the fuse caught and using a sweeping backhand Burkhart slung the burning stick over and up.

The explosion was deafening but the concussion blasted over the top of his hole, having no effect. Grabbing saddlebags and rifle, he instantly threw himself over the far edge of his wall and, rolling to his feet, sprinted into the darkness.

Just as it seemed he was free of danger, someone spoke loudly off to his left. In what must have been Arabic, another voice answered hysterically from the direction of the fox hole.

Abruptly, Burkhart cut to the right and dove for the ground, but an eruption of bullets burned a white-hot streak across his back and tore the rifle from his hand. Then, as suddenly as it had started, it stopped, leaving only the two foreign tongues calling cautiously back and forth through the blackness of night.

After a short but futile search for the Winchester, Burkhart began crawling quietly but rapidly through the sage putting distance between himself and the voices. Stopping occasionally to listen, he was certain he was not being followed. Even though he could understand nothing of what was being said, he surmised the rear guard must have been one of the two he had wounded earlier and either could not or, would not, continue the search in the dark.

After going a quarter mile on all fours, Burkhart stopped and listened intently for any sound, any hint of pursuit, for a long five minutes. Hearing nothing but the gentle rustling of sage in the last breaths of evening wind, he stood and tossed the saddlebags over his shoulder. When the rear pouch slammed into his back he grimaced painfully.

Reaching behind him, he tugged at the wetness in his shirt and brought his hand back around. Even in the starlight he saw the blood. Stooping to examine the light colored sand he saw it there too. They would have no trouble finding his trail in the morning!

CHAPTER FIFTEEN

Making the last three miles in the daylight would have been child's play, but in the moonless night Burkhart had to move slower. Unable to distinguish any landmarks, he did not find the quarter acre knoll of dead junipers until morning.

Weakened and lightheaded from loss of blood, he uncovered the canteen he had cached the week before and leaned against a boulder to rest. After sipping slowly from the canteen he took some jerked beef from his saddlebags and took a bite. It would be at least an hour before they would find him, but he had finally stopped bleeding. The salted meat and water would at least have some time to help him recover.

The terrain had changed slightly, being more rocky with stands of thicker sage and juniper on a few of the low hills. To his rear and just above him was a pile of mine tailings leading up to an abandoned shaft that went no more than thirty feet into the slope. On the roof of the mine entrance, he wedged the second stick of dynamite into the rocks then cut the fuse to six inches.

Facing Eagle butte, now several miles to the southeast, the sun was beginning to rise on his left, but it had not cleared the horizon before he saw two figures moving swiftly towards him. And from the careless way they advanced, it was clear his lost rifle had been discovered and they were confidently closing in for the kill.

Before climbing into the dense thicket of dead branches, lava rock and stumps, Burkhart meticulously scanned the desert in every direction for the other men. Had they flanked him without his knowing it? Were they on the other side of the hill behind him, or were they even closer?

Unable to take anymore time, he slipped through the dried undergrowth then went to his knees crawling over the rocks as he worked his way into the thickest part of the brittle forest. It would be close work, yet with only a pistol for defense, maneuverability was his only advantage. But, he realized gravely, their automatic weapons were scarcely more cumbersome than his Colt.

A moment after sliding uncomfortably between a pair of large rocks, he caught the end of a muffled conversation and the soft crunch of boots being carefully placed on the gritty soil.

Circling around him, at least for now, Burkhart heard only two men. The others, wherever they were, did not concern him. The sounds from his perimeter told him this pair of gunmen had already discovered his position.

"Hear me, Jason Burkhart," called out a voice in near perfect English. "You are to be executed for the murder of our brothers of Greater Syria. You will be an example of our ability to strike at the very core of the Great Satan. Your death will strike fear in the hearts of all infidels."

From deep within the thicket, Burkhart grunted indignantly then shouted, "Is that so? You're the ones that are thirsty and trapped in the middle of the desert with no hope of escape."

Instantly, bullets rattled harmlessly through the branches above him but were halted by a booming command. Then more calmly and with the pompous fervor of a fanatic, the commander resumed. "Our deaths mean nothing! We are honored to die for Allah! We are only the first of many that will afflict the Zionist until there is a greater Syria. This land will be stained with our blood, but it will run deep with yours."

Following another order in Arabic, Burkhart heard small branches snapping ahead of him and readied for a frontal attack but a minute later, he knew it would not come. They were building a fire!

In a few heartbeats, a few rapid, pounding heartbeats, the popping changed to a crackling, then quickly to a roar. Instinctively Burkhart made his decision and started for the edge of the junipers. He would not wait to be flushed like a rabbit and then be slaughtered. He was tired of running, tired of hiding. It was not a thought; it was a reflex. He would attack!

With the noise of the inferno covering him, Burkhart moved quickly until he could make out one of the terrorists, then paused and crept closer to the edge of the thicket. Squatting on his heels and feeling the heat of the oncoming blaze, he grabbed a large piece of lava rock, and in a low arc threw it hard further down the slope into the unburned brush.

Rushing towards the crashing sound, the guard turned his back and Burkhart lunged forward bursting into the clear. Jerking to a stop, he forced himself to take his time and center the front blade of the Colt squarely between the shoulder blades of his target.

The gunman spun as the revolver leveled, but now with the sights resting squarely in the middle of his chest, Burkhart squeezed the trigger. The .45 bucked sharply in his palm, but was followed by a single, heavier blast to his rear.

Twisting and diving to his right, Burkhart rolled on his shoulder and instantly came up on one knee with the pistol cocked and ready to fire. But sixty feet away, wearing a metal knee-brace and pointing the large bore of a shotgun at him, stood the sheriff! Between them lay the second terrorist, his back shredded by buckshot.

A glance over his shoulder told Burkhart that his .45 slug had done the job intended, and he eased the hammer down on his Colt. Standing slowly, he curiously stared at Muller but kept his pistol leveled.

The sheriff took a few steps forward and nudged the corps with the barrel of his shotgun then rolled it over with his foot. When he raised his head to look back at Burkhart, his eyes flickered with some hidden thought, narrowing into sinister slits as a veil of evil spread over his face.

Sharpened by the ordeal of the last two weeks, Burkhart's senses were honed to a primordial keenness, and his thumb slid up and over to rest on the hammer of his pistol. "You can explain my death, Muller," said Burkhart warningly …"but not if I'm full of buckshot."

Jolted by Burkhart's insight, Muller's expression gradually mutated into a hateful sneer. As if murder had never crossed his mind, he lazily shouldered the scattergun. "I came out here to take you in, Burkhart! I've got the extradition papers and you're under arrest."

Turning his head, Burkhart looked at the flames and watched the fire scorch the sky, a sky already pale from the suns heat. Holstering his colt, he said coolly, "Now, you'll be on their list , Sheriff. And once you're on it, you can't get off."

"What list?" growled Muller over the rumbling blaze. "What are you trying to pull this time?"

Pointing to the dead man at his feet Burkhart replied, "Their list. Like me, you'll be a marked man if you take me in now. You killed one of them, too. You'll get all the credit."

The sheriff's brow furrowed deeply, his expression suddenly changing. But before he could reply, Burkhart continued. "And we better not stand here in the open. There's three more of them out there somewhere."

The sheriff waved a disregarding hand. "Yeah, there were three, alright. You left a trail of bodies behind you that a blind man could follow. Horses and men…or what's left of them."

"How did you get here?" asked Burkhart. "Ride or drive?"

"The Blazer. It's parked over the rise," answered Muller stepping away from the heat of the fire. For a long minute he chewed nervously at the inside of his cheek and stared at the body in front of him. Then, after a disgusted snort, he glanced up. "What do you have in mind?"

"Go back and get the bodies and bring them back here."

Muller stared blankly at Burkhart but slowly the same idea began to form in his head. "Hell, one of them is in pieces. What'd you do to him?"

"Never mind about that. You have a body bag don't you?"

"Yeah," muttered Muller distastefully.

"Well, I'm sure you know the pieces we need to get rid of. Leave the rest if you want. We don't want anything that can be identified back there."

Swearing disgustedly, Muller turned and walked away stopping only to glare back at the two dead men before he disappeared over the hill. When Burkhart saw the dust of the truck driving away, he began dragging the bodies up the slope and into the rear of the mineshaft. He then returned to the edge of the flaming thicket and picked up the weapons and all the empty casings he could find. He wanted nothing left behind. They were to merely vanish and never be seen or heard of again. There would be no prisoners, no hostages, no press coverage and no propaganda. It would end quietly, uneventfully and without martyrdom. And perhaps, without escalation.

An hour later, Muller drove past the smoldering ashes and up to where Burkhart sat waiting. "Now what," he asked guardedly. "I'm not digging any graves."

"Put it in reverse and back up to that mine up there," answered Burkhart pointing to the shaft. "They go in there with the others. Did you find their guns?"

"Only two. I was going to keep them myself," offered Muller.

"You think it's worth the risk?" snapped Burkhart. "You know the FBI will be in on this. And those guns may have left a paper trail. You know that better than I do."

"Alright!" blurted Muller, "Have it your way."

After the two bodies and half filled body bag were in place, Burkhart and Muller walked out into the sunlight, both uneasy with the task they had completed.

"We going to bury them or what?" asked the pale sheriff as he wiped two clammy palms on the front of his pants.

"Sort of," replied Burkhart then picked up a smoking juniper he had brought up from below. "You better move the truck back a hundred or so yards."

"What for?"

"Dynamite."

"Dynamite!" exclaimed Muller, his eyes widening. "So that's what happened to that guy."

Holding the partially burned branch, Burkhart blew on the glowing tip to keep it alive. "I didn't know until you told me. It was dark. I was just trying to get away from them."

"Served them right, Burkhart. They got what they deserved."

"Maybe so, but at least they came at me in a stand up fight. That's more than most of them do."

As Burkhart neared the dynamite Muller started the truck. Leaning out the window he said flatly, "You're still under arrest."

"Whatever," sighed Burkhart and touched the fuse with the amber. Muller yelped and gunned the engine as Burkhart ran horizontally across the slope away from the mine's entrance. Counting to himself, he hit the ground just as the desert shook from the blast and debris exploded up and away from the hillside covering the area in a huge cloud of dust.

When Burkhart came back down the slope, Muller was waiting and leaning against the shady side of his truck. “Glad to see you made it,” he said then drew his revolver from its holster. “I’ll take that pistol of yours…right now!”

Holding his hands up as Muller took the Colt, Burkhart glanced over the big man’s shoulder. “It would look better at that,” he said easily. “We’ve got company.”

“Sure we do,” mocked the sheriff then took the belt as well. “Hands on the top of the truck and spread your legs.”

As the handcuff’s snapped tightly around Burkhart’s wrists, a distant drum-like rumbling began to fill the sky and was growing louder by the second.

“What now!” howled Muller as he looked up to see a large helicopter coming directly towards them. “What the hell is that?”

Flying over them before making a sharp turn, the helicopter circled slowly a half dozen times in an increasingly wider circle. After completing what seemed to be a search of the area, it returned to land in a mechanical sand storm a few yards away from the Blazer.

Emerging first from the open doors were two men in dark business suits holding automatic rifles. A third hopped down from the body of the chopper as a forth person opened the cockpit door and stepped out. It was Kimberly!

Running past the men she threw her arms around Jason holding, her head against his chest. “Thank God you’re alright, Jason Burkhart. I was so afraid.”

With his hands locked behind him and unsure of what to do or say, Burkhart hesitated, glancing first at Muller then to the stranger approaching from the helicopter.

The man coming towards him wore a faint smile. “Hello, Burkhart. So we meet again.”

Burkhart looked at the suit and thought of what Mac had told him about the airport. “Agent Mader?”

"That's right."

Burkhart nodded then shrugged, "Find your van?"

"Sure did. But there's a rental car we've yet to locate."

Kimberly pulled away now smiling at the conversation between the two men and slid her arm into Burkhart's and held him with the other.

"Who are you?" demanded Muller with eyes full of antagonism. "How'd you find us?"

"Special Agent in Charge, Mader, FBI. We'd been searching for an hour before we saw the cloud of dust and decided to take a look."

"Well," bellowed Muller defiantly, "you're too late. I already made the arrest."

Mader ignored the boast and took a casual look around. His eyes drifted to the fresh depression on the slope where the mine used to be. "Have a fire did you?"

Muller's expression softened suddenly, and with his voice more at ease he said, "He was hiding in the brush. I had to burn it to get him out."

"You what!" exclaimed Kimberly.

"He had a gun," pleaded Muller as he defensively pointed to the pistol and belt on the front seat of his truck.

"Is that true, Jason?"

"I'll have to take the fifth on that," answered Burkhart trying not to look into her eyes.

Still holding him she looked steadily at Bob Muller. "Well…I'm sure he had a good reason for anything he might have done."

"By the way," interrupted Mader casually, "your friend McWilliams says to say he's fine."

Visibly stunned, Burkhart glanced down at Kimberly. "Mac's alive?"

"That's why we're here, Jason. Yesterday after they left him on the side of the road, he regained consciousness and made it to my ranch. Then we called Agent Mader."

Still confused, Burkhart shook his head. "Called him about what?"

"Travis thought they were Mexicans with a broken down car. They flagged him down and then hit him over the head."

"Who did?" asked Burkhart slowly beginning to understand.

"Before they hit him," broke in Mader, "he heard enough to know they weren't speaking Spanish. He put it together who they were. We knew they were in the country but we lost track of them at the last minute. They're a splinter group of the Hezbollah, Party of God. And we had reason to believe they were here for you. When McWilliams called, we knew for sure."

Mader hesitated, then reached down and picked up a partially buried shell casing. Blowing the dust from it, he took a closer look and smelled the open end. After a calculating glance up the slope and a long unbelieving look at Burkhart, he tossed it deep into the sage. "I'm afraid you were the victim of politics. At first we were told to hold back…to keep our distance from you."

"Why?"

"I can only guess, but I believe you were to be allowed to be killed, a sacrifice for peace sort of. They were hoping to avoid an all out terrorist campaign in the United States by allowing the Muslims their revenge. At least it seems that way to me."

Neither Muller, Kimberly nor Burkhart replied as they glanced one to another in unbelieving shock.

"But after you shot up those news cameras," continued Mader, "and then ran them off your land, things changed. We had one of our people in that group and after the chief got her report, he took it on his own to bury the story in the name of National Security. What you did impressed him Burkhart. And it apparently woke up a lot of people in some very high places."

Muller scowled suspiciously. "What are you getting at, Mader,"

"What it boils down to…Sheriff…is that you may take the handcuffs off of him. He is in Federal custody now. It's over."

Muller's face flushed red as the veins crossing his temples began to bulge. After a long, hard look at Kimberly, he jerked the keys from his pocket and tossed them at Mader's feet. "He's your prisoner, so you take them off!" he snarled then slammed the door of his truck and without a look back, sped out across the desert.

"He's got my Colt in there," said Burkhart as Mader freed his hands.

Mader winked at Kimberly. "We'll get it back to you," he said and with an understanding grin added, "I'll be over at the helicopter."

Burkhart watched the agent walk away and suddenly felt Kimberly taking both his hands. "Jason," she began softly, "it's going to be alright. Mac talked to me…about you…and me. Everything is going to be fine. It is over."

"How can it be, Kimberly?" asked Jason, allowing himself a look into her dark brown eyes. "They won't give up. I can't be sure of that, at least not sure enough to…"

Putting her fingers to his lips she said, "There's a program for you, Jason. You'll have a new identity, a new life. A new beginning."

Jason gently took her hand down and held it. "I can't have that and stay around here. And I had hoped…I thought a new beginning was possible…But you were part of that hope…And I'm not ready to give that up."

Smiling broadly, Kimberly put her hands around his neck and pulled him to her. Kissing him affectionately she leaned back, and placed his arms around her. "I was praying you would feel that way," she said with a warm glow. "How do you feel about Colorado?"

Jason shook his head. "Kimberly, I'm not following you very well."

Kimberly laughed happily. "Don't worry. You don't have to follow me, we'll go together."

"Where?"

"To Colorado, dear! My uncle has been wanting me to take over his ranch for years. We can sell both our places here and double its size. It will be a good life for us, Jason. We can start over… together."

Jason Burkhart studied the beautiful face in front of him. "A second chance," he sighed wearily. "I've been working on that for a long time …But moving again…and changing my name…That will take some getting used to."

"I don't know about that," returned Kimberly wryly. "Us women have to do it all the time."

"You've got a good point there," admitted Jason breaking into a faint grin. "What would my new name be?"

With a playful smile Kimberly whispered, "How do you feel about Whitney?"

Pulling her closer to him he kissed her gently. "I think I fell in love with that name the first time I heard it."

www.ingramcontent.com/pod-product-compliance
Lightning Source LLC
Chambersburg PA
CBHW030315180626
46810CB00003B/1094

* 9 7 8 1 6 2 5 5 0 4 7 1 5 *